HANNAH THE HEALER

COWBOYS AND ANGELS

GEORGE MCVEY

Copyright © 2017 by George H. McVey All rights reserved.

Cover design by Erin Dameron Hill/ EDH Graphics

No part of this book may be reproduced in any form or by any electronic or mechanical means including information storage and retrieval systems, without permission in writing from the author. The only exception is by a reviewer, who may quote short excerpts in a review.

This book is a work of fiction. Names, characters, places, and incidents either are products of the author's imagination or are used fictitiously. Any resemblance to actual persons, living or dead, events, or locales is entirely coincidental or used fictitiously.

To my family. You put up with me sequestered in my writer's cave and hardly ever complain as I bring these characters and stories to life. Know that I love each one of you and thank God for you daily. Even if I am grumpy at times.

1

Hannah Coppersmith sat upright in bed, surprised by the woman standing at the foot. The woman, who was dressed in an expensive dinner dress and had her auburn hair streaked with grey pinned under a stylish hat, had just appeared out of thin air. "Hello dear, don't be afraid. I would have tried not to make such a dramatic entrance if we had more time, but we don't. I need you to come with me or that young man you've loved forever is going to die tonight."

Hannah stopped trying to figure out who this woman was and what she meant; there was only one person her heart ever wanted and she had been surprised when he'd ridden up to her cabin several months ago astride a golden palomino with the star of a U.S. Marshal pinned to his chest. If this strange woman said Henry Wheeler was going to die without her then she would follow the stranger to the end of the earth, or at least as far as her legs would take her.

"Get your medical supplies, dear, and a goodly amount of bandage wraps. I would have gone for that doctor you work for, but he's gonna have his hands full tonight with that self-important Reverend your man's saving."

"Henry isn't my man; he doesn't even remember who I am."

The woman gave a regal smile. "That don't make him any less yours, just means he ain't realized you're his yet. We'll see that he does." Then the woman winked. "Now hurry, dear, he's about to need you to save his life."

Hannah grabbed her medical bag, added the extra bandages, and followed the woman out of her cabin. Her buggy was hitched and the woman climbed up and took the reins. Hannah climbed up beside her. "Where are we going?"

"It seems some of the townspeople decided to hang them a preacher, and the young Marshal is going to put a stop to it. We're heading out toward the mine where the Marshal will be laying on the ground bleeding out. You need to be prepared, Hannah. It's going to be bad at first. But have no fear, it is not his appointed time to meet the angel of death. You have seen to that by following me in faith."

As they drew closer to the run up to Bachelor and the mines beyond, sure enough, Hannah saw Henry's horse standing by the side of the road. Henry lay in the middle of the road and a dark hooded figure stood over him. The hooded figure was as black as night except for his glowing red eyes. The woman pulled the buggy to a stop and jumped toward the figure before the wheels had stopped moving. "You go on now. I brought her, you're not needed here. Go on and get now."

The angel of death nodded once, and then dark wings spread from his back and he soared straight up into the air. Hannah quickly approached the figure on the ground. Sure enough, it was Marshal Wheeler, as if there had been any doubt. It was too dark for her to figure out where he was bleeding from. "I need light; why didn't you tell me to bring a lantern?"

The woman just chuckled. Suddenly the area around her started to glow until Hannah could see Henry well enough to know the blood was coming from a gunshot wound on his back. It wasn't dead center; she was pretty sure that it had missed his spine but the amount of blood was troublesome. Hannah grabbed the scissors from her bag and cut his coat and shirt away from the wound. She didn't want to move him any more than necessary until she got the bleeding stopped. She pressed on the wound and heard him moan. "Henry, hold still, I know it hurts but I've got to stop the bleeding."

She knew that he wasn't really aware, but he looked right at her and his face lit up. "Esther is that you? Have you come back to me?"

She sucked in a breath. He thought she was her sister, the woman he'd pined over even after she married another man. Her mysterious visitor was wrong; he wasn't hers, he never had been, even now after her death he belonged to her older, prettier sister. She got the bleeding stopped and knew she needed to get him back to her place and remove the bullet. Hannah knew she couldn't move him alone. Henry was too heavy for her to lift alone. She looked up at the stranger only to notice that the glow around her faded with each passing second. "I need to get him into the buggy. I don't know how we're going to accomplish that."

The stranger smiled as two men in white robes shining as brightly as she had earlier suddenly appeared. "I got that covered, my dear. You just tie his horse to the back of the buggy and I'll have him ready when you are."

Hannah watched as the two men she couldn't deny were

angels picked up Henry and laid him as gentle as a newborn on the back seat of her buggy. She quickly tied his mount to the back and climbed in the buggy only to realize that suddenly she was all alone with Henry Wheeler lying on her back buggy seat. She turned the buggy in the wide spot and hurried back to her cabin. She needed to get the bullet out and clean and dress the wound quickly before infection could set in. She'd take time to think about the miraculous visitations once Henry was out of danger.

Newly appointed U.S. Marshal Henry Wheeler was heading back from the Bonanza Claim Mine late on New Year's Eve. He'd gone chasing a rumor that one of the miners might have information for him about the connection between Archie Grady, Sheriff Ketchem and the kidnapped women. The rumor had turned out to be just that, a rumor. However, it wasn't a complete waste of time. While not being able to pin Archibald Grady to the kidnappings, he had gathered some more evidence of Ketchem's being a bought man. He couldn't connect the sheriff directly to Grady, but there was more evidence of him being connected to Mr. Anders, Archie's rich uncle and the owner of the Bonanza Claim Mine and several other businesses in Creede and Bachelor.

He was just coming through Creede heading back to his small space above the Marshal's office in Topaz, when he saw several torches and heard angry voices off to the right just about the tree line. He'd not figured to run into too many people tonight. He figured those miners with money would all be at the Golden Nugget or one of the other saloon tents celebrating the new year with whiskey and soiled doves. What in the world would have that many people gathered outside town in the dark?

He turned his mount toward the ruckus and rode right up on what appeared to be a bunch of miners and other men from town in the process of lynching the Reverend Eugene Theodore. Henry quietly pulled his Henry Repeater from the rifle boot on his saddle and held it across his lap. No one paid any attention to him as he stopped just outside the circle of the lynch mob. He could hear Reverend Theodore from where he was as he tried to scare the mob into turning him loose.

"You are in danger of damning your souls to hell. Why would you do that? Turn from this wickedness you've set yourself on."

Most of the men from the mines just laughed, but it was the men with bandanas covering the lower half of their faces that Henry concentrated on. In particular, the one nearest the horse the Preacher sat on with the noose around his neck. That man looked familiar to Henry. He was almost positive that it was Archie Grady. The man on the other side, also with a mask on his face, leaned toward the Bible thumper and spoke. "Well now, Reverend, according to you every man here is going to hell anyway. You said those that gambled, drank whiskey, got drunk, and slept with the whores at the Nugget were all going to hell. That's every man here, so what's a little murder gonna do?"

That was Henry's cue and he lifted the rifle and worked the lever as he spoke. "It might send ya there quicker, that's for certain. I guarantee you that you two beside the Reverend will definitely be there tonight if you try to hang the man."

"What gives you the right to interfere with us, mister?"

Henry pulled his wool and lamb's fur coat open so that

his shiny Marshal badge was visible. "Reckon we ain't met yet. Names Wheeler, United States Marshal Henry Wheeler to be exact, and what you and these other men are doing is against the law. Take the noose off the Reverend or the first bullet I fire goes into you."

As he was talking, several of the miners had started to slip off into the darkness. Henry figured that they didn't want to end up recognized and arrested by a U.S. Marshal. Before things could get any tenser, there came the sound of a horse being ridden hard coming up behind Henry. He half turned and saw Sheriff Ketchem racing toward them. Movement in front of him caused him to look forward and see the two men who he had pegged as the leaders riding away, leaving the Reverend, noose still around his neck, sitting on a yellow nag all alone. Ketchem rode up beside Wheeler. "What's going on here, Marshal?"

"Sheriff, it seems that some of the good citizens of Creede took it upon themselves to hang the preacher for speaking out against their way of living."

"Guess we should go set him free before we try to catch any of the lynch mob."

"I reckon so. I did recognize Archie's voice as one of the men actually holding the preacher on the horse."

The sheriff sighed. "I know you don't want to hear this, but you're gonna need more than a voice you think was his to tie him to this."

Henry looked at Ketchem, "One day soon, sheriff, you're gonna have to decide if you are a lawman or Anders' paid enforcer."

"Now see here! I resent that you and everyone else thinks I'm giving Mr. Anders and Mr. Grady a pass on obeying the law."

Wheeler shook his head and moved his horse to go take

the noose off Eugene and cut him free. He'd gone a few feet when there was the crack of a small gun and a sharp pain to his back. He heard Sheriff Ketchem call out that someone was shooting at them and fire his Colt behind them which caused the Reverend's horse to spook and take off, leaving the good Reverend swinging by his neck on the noose. Henry tried to lift the rifle to shoot the rope but his right arm wouldn't move. He quickly drew his Peacemaker with his left hand, and thanked God for Nathan insisting that he practice accuracy and speed with both hands every day for the last four years. He sighted on the rope where it came over the tree limb and fired. Eugene dropped to the ground and sat there coughing and retching. Ketchem rode up with Henry to where the minister sat stunned on the ground. "Looks like we need to get the Reverend here to see the Doc."

Henry ignored the pain in his back and the way his right side was going numb. "You do that. I'll follow you."

Ketchem looked at him. "You okay?"

"I'll be all right. Might let the doc know I'm gonna need his services, too. Seems that shot might have hit me."

Ketchem looked at the Marshal, a look of concern on his face. "You sure you want me to leave ya?"

"Get Eugene to the Doc. I'll make it."

The sheriff got down, cut the Reverend's hands free and took the noose off his neck. Then he put him behind his saddle, climbed on and headed for the doctor's cabin on the other side of Creede close to Bachelor. Henry knew he wouldn't be able to make that ride; he could feel the numbness creeping through his body. It was closer to Hannah Coppersmith's place. He'd just have to pray she wasn't out delivering a baby somewhere. He headed that way as snow began to fall. New Year's Eve just wasn't gonna ever be a good night for him, apparently. He started toward Topaz and the nurse's small shack she was renting from Waylon Morgan. He had reached the turn off to the line shack when the numbness caught up with him and he felt himself sliding out of the saddle. His vision started to grey out as his body slammed onto the frozen trail. He thought he might be dying as the last thing he saw was a middle-aged woman in a fancy dress looking down at him with a dark shadowy figure with red eyes beside her. "You keep watch, but don't you take him, you hear me? It's not his appointed time." He thought he saw the shadow nod, but everything went black as the numbness slipped over him completely.

2

Hannah pulled up in front of her cabin and instantly started to fret. Henry was pale, almost to the point of looking gray, and still out from blood loss. There was no way to get him inside to remove the bullet. She couldn't lift him, he weighed about a hundred and fifty pounds more than she did. She climbed out of the buggy and looked up at the sky. "I could use some help here, God."

Her cabin door opened and out came the same woman who had disappeared on her earlier. "You just have to ask, child. You know what the good book says: You have not because you ask not." The woman took one of Henry's arms and pointed Hannah to the other one. "You grab that side and between us I think we can drag him in and onto your bed. I took the liberty of putting the oil cloths down to keep from ruining your sheets and ticking. I also have the instruments and needles you'll need in a pan of boiling water."

Hannah stared at the woman for a moment before moving to do what she'd said. As they dragged Henry into her little home and over to the bed, Hannah wondered about the woman. Something about her seemed so familiar. "Do I know you?"

The older woman smiled at her. "I wondered if you'd recognize me. Yes, dear, I knew you when you were a bit younger. You and my granddaughter used to come over and have tea with me once in a while, both at the house and in our private Pullman."

Hannah gasped. "Mrs. Ryder? But I thought Elizabeth said you'd passed somewhere out in New Mexico."

The older woman smiled. "It's Penelope, dear, or Penny if you prefer. While I may have passed on from my life in this world, the Creator does allow me and that old mountain man I married an occasional adventure. You and Marshal Wheeler are my assignment this time around. I believe you would call me your guardian angel, even though I'm not really an angel. So if you need me, you just ask and I'll come calling."

Together they laid Henry on the bed and Hannah quickly tore the hole she'd cut earlier removing both his coat and shirt without turning him over. She pulled the instruments that Penny had boiled out of the water and stuck them in a small basin of medicinal alcohol to finish sterilizing them. She rinsed her hands in the alcohol as well and then went to work. First, she removed the bandage she'd used to stop the blood flow, and then gently cleaned the drying blood from around the wound. She flushed it with some of the alcohol and once she had it as clean as she could, she grabbed the tweezers and started trying to pull out the bullet. She felt the metal of the tweezers grip the lead slug and slowly started extracting it. Henry groaned and she stopped pulling. She needed to be careful. Though she'd assisted Doctor Thomas removing a slug several times and had even had to do a few herself, they had never been this close to the spine.

Hannah was afraid that Henry would wake and jerk and cause her to push the bullet, tweezers, or both into his spinal cord and do him serious damage. She wished she had some ether to make sure he was good and out, but all she had going for her was blood loss and pain. While she needed to be careful, she needed to be quick, too, before he did wake up and cause more damage to himself. She resumed pulling with slow steady pressure and in a few quick minutes that felt like forever, she had the slug resting in the dish of alcohol. It was smaller than the bullets she'd pulled out of other men, but not as small as the bird shot she'd had to remove from one of the miners who'd gotten crosswise of the Widow Sanderson.

She quickly poured more alcohol into the wound to clean it out as much as possible, used a clean bandage to remove the excess from the wound, and stitched it up. Finally, she put a fresh bandage on it. Henry hadn't awakened yet and that worried her. He'd lost a lot of blood. If he woke and she could get some blood-building foods in him and he didn't get an infection, then she'd breathe easier. She turned to see the angel of her childhood friend's grandmother watching her. "You did good, dear. Now you have another choice to make."

Hannah frowned, "What choice?"

"There's a blizzard coming. I know it's snowed steady since Christmas, but what's coming will make travel impossible for a while after. So here's your choice. Be trapped here for the better part of a week with your young man, just the two of you alone in this shelter. You know what that will lead to when people find out. Or we can load him back in the buggy and take him over to Doctor Thomas's cabin. You'll be snowed in here alone then."

Hannah didn't even think, she knew what would happen when Reverend Bing and Reverend Theodore found out they'd been alone for a week. She'd get her dream come true and be Henry's wife. She just prayed in time her angel would be right and he'd come to truly be hers. "I don't think we should move him again. He's too weak, another trip might just kill him."

Penny smiled. "Of course, dear. You're the one with the medical training; I'm sure you know best. Now he'll wake in the morning and you'll have seven days before anyone will get out here to you. I think I'll make sure you have a chaperone, though, to keep things from getting too intimate."

"A chaperone?" Hannah's face fell. If someone else was trapped with them, then her plan wouldn't work.

Penny laughed. "Don't worry, dear, this chaperone won't derail your plan. Just make sure Marshal Wheeler doesn't get amorous and anticipate the wedding night."

Penny walked to the door and opened it. In strutted a black and brown Rhode Island Red rooster with a bright red comb and wattle. He strutted in and right over to Hannah, clucking as he came. The angel smiled. "That's Bob. He's an attack chicken and he knows he's to keep you and your virtue safe."

Hannah couldn't help but laugh. "A rooster? The thing you choose to protect my virtue is a rooster?"

"Bob is a very special rooster. You'll see, he'll let you and your lawman get to know each other but not get too close. Plus, he's good company. You can talk to him and he never shares your secrets." Penny looked down at the bird. "Keep Hannah safe, Bob."

The rooster clucked and then crowed as if to say he'd see

to it. Penny nodded and stepped out the door. "Remember, Hannah, if you need me just call out to God and ask for me. I'll be around." Then she was gone and the door shut on its own. Hannah looked down at the rooster. "Well, Bob, guess it's just you and me and the man with a hole in his back."

The bird tilted his head first one way and then the other before giving a quiet cluck and walking over to the bed and looking at Henry lying there. Hannah went over and pulled Marshal Wheeler's arms out of the shirt and coat she'd slit up the back and removed them both to make him more comfortable. She needed to get him off the oil cloth so she could wash it and hang it to dry in case she had need of it again. She knew Penny had told her she'd be alone without anyone for the next seven days, but it was ingrained in her to keep her birthing and doctoring kit ready. She rolled the oil cloth until it was bunched against Henry's flesh, and then she rolled the unconscious Marshal over onto his left side and rolled the oil cloth up against his front. She carefully lowered him back onto his stomach, rolled him onto his right side, and finished rolling the oilcloth. She lowered him back onto his stomach and pulled the roll off the foot of the bed. She quickly wiped it clean and hung it over her table to dry. Then she stoked the fire in the fireplace and the cook stove to keep the cabin warm and made herself a pile of blankets and quilts to sleep on. She quickly changed into her nightgown and slid under a quilt. Once she was covered, Bob came over and roosted at her feet. She quickly slipped into sleep knowing she'd have a full day tomorrow caring for Henry Wheeler.

∼

HENRY KNEW HE WAS DREAMING. He remembered getting

shot and trying to get to Hannah Coppersmith's cabin. But now he was reliving another New Year's Eve, the one five years ago when he'd asked Esther to be his wife at her family's party.

The strawberry blonde with the bluest eyes he'd ever seen had laughed at him on his knee holding up a ring to her. "Get up, Henry. You can't be serious."

He frowned. "I'm very serious, Esther. I love you and want you to be my wife."

She shook her head. "No, that's not possible. Surely you know you were just a bit of fun for me while I waited for Augustus to make up his mind. He did today. He asked me to become Mrs. Rayner over lunch and I said yes."

Henry stood and slipped the ring in his pocket. "I see, and yet tonight you let me attend your parents' ball. Why? To make fun of me?"

She shook her head. "Of course not, Henry. You've been a good friend. I wanted to share my joy with you."

Henry looked at her and saw the laughter she was trying to hide in her eyes. "I see. One last bit of fun with ole Henry. Well, when you wake up and realize that my love is better than Rayner's money, it might just be too late, Esther."

He turned to leave. "Don't be like that, Henry. Why don't you go and ask Hannah to dance, it would make her night."

Henry looked across the ballroom where the younger Coppersmith sister sat all alone. Hannah, the one who everyone knew was going to go to college and become a nurse. She talked of nothing else. She was set to start at the end of January. "I don't think so. Give my regrets to your family for me."

With that, he left not just the ball but the entire house. He knew he was being rude but he didn't care. He got outside and went to fetch a handsome cab when Augustus

Rayner came up beside him. "She's mine now, Wheeler. Make sure and stay away from her or I'll have to teach you respect."

Henry looked at the man. He was two years older than both himself and Esther. "You have nothing to worry about, Rayner. I know where I'm not wanted."

"See that you do." The older man clapped him on the shoulder, squeezing to try and bring him to his knees, but Henry Wheeler was nothing if not tough and proud. He stood, vowing never to kneel before the rich dandy. Instead, he nodded and pulled away as a cab stopped for him. "The Brooklyn Club."

He spent the rest of the night drowning his sorrows in cheap whiskey. When he finally woke in the morning, he was lying on his bed, a flyer clutched in his hand. "Wanted: young men looking for adventure. Become a member of the United States Marshal Service." It gave an address in the Wall Street district. The longer Henry looked at it the more it appealed to him. A life of adventure chasing criminals. NO lying women in sight. He stood, and when he was sure he could remain standing, he headed for the office of the U.S. Marshal Service to sign up as a deputy marshal.

His dream changed and he lay on the frozen ground, snow falling all around him again. When Esther looked down on him, he called out to her and suddenly she changed and was Hannah. Hannah, whose cabin he was heading for when he'd passed out. But where was his beloved Esther? Why hadn't she loved him like he loved her? Five years and more than halfway across the country and she still filled his mind. She always would be the woman he loved, even if she never loved him back. Then gratefully he moaned, and a quiet voice lifted his head and poured a small amount of a bitter liquid into his mouth. "Swallow, Henry, this will ease the pain and let you rest."

He did as he was told and slipped back into the blackness from before. All his pain, both in his back and his heart, slipped away into the blackness as well.

3
―――

Henry woke warm but in pain, the smell of bacon and coffee filtered through the pain in his back. He started to sit up and that caused the pain in his back to increase and he sucked in a sharp breath, which caused the woman at the cook stove to turn. "So Marshal, you're awake. Please stay in the bed; you came very close to dying last night. You lost a lot of blood and the bullet that hit you missed your spine by a mere couple of inches."

The vision before him was indeed Hannah Coppersmith, Esther's little sister all grown up. "I made it then?"

She turned and looked at him, and his body reacted. When had little Hannah become this beautiful woman in front of him. The glow from the fireplace to her side and the lantern behind her had her hair blazing in the colors of sunset: orange, red, yellow, gold all mixed together. Her gray eyes brought to mind the sky just after a storm before the sun emerged and turned it blue, full of passion and spent fury. The dress and simple white apron she wore did nothing to hide the womanly curves in all Henry's favorite places. He was again reminded that this wasn't the wallflower he'd last seen in New York. No, this woman was all woman. "What do you mean, you made it then?"

Henry tried to pull himself upright in the bed but once again the pain was more than he could bear and he lay back on the bed. "I was trying to get here last night after I knew I was shot. I knew I couldn't make it to the Doc's place on the far side of Creede."

She walked over to him with a plate of eggs and bacon. "For your information, you didn't make it. I found you in the middle of the road about two miles from here at the turnoff to Topaz. Your horse standing over you."

"How did I get here then?"

"I got you in my buggy and brought you here, then I removed the bullet and cleaned your wound. I ended up destroying your coat and shirt. However, I thought keeping you alive was more important. Now let me help you sit up slowly so you can eat. You're going to be very weak for a while. You lost a lot of blood."

"I need to get out of here and check on Reverend Theodore."

The nurse easily stopped him from trying to stand. Henry was surprised at how little effort it took her to restrain him. She was right; he was very weak.

"You aren't going anywhere, Marshal. Not only are you weak as a newborn, there is a major blizzard blowing outside. You wouldn't even make it to the end of my yard without getting lost in the white out."

"That's not good, you know what people will say when they find out we were snowed in together alone. You should have taken me to Doctor Thomas when you found me."

Hannah's hands turned into fists sitting against her waist. "You wouldn't have lasted to Doctor Thomas's place. You almost didn't last till I got you here. When I found you it was like death was standing over you, waiting to snatch you at a moment's notice."

Henry shook his head. "But your reputation. Hannah, what will everyone think after this?"

Henry watched as she glared down at him. "Do you really care, Henry Wheeler? Because it would be the first time you cared about me."

"That's not true. I care about you. I care about all you young ladies that were kidnapped. Why do you think I was out and about last night? You of all people should know how I feel about New Year's Eve."

Hannah's eyes flashed with anger and Henry was almost certain he could see the storm clouds building in the gray sky of her eyes. "That's right, because of Esther. Is that why you're worried, because I was Esther's little sister?"

"You know that's not true; she chose someone else. I don't care what she thinks of me anymore. However, I don't want her to accuse me of destroying you to get back at her."

Hannah gasped and started to cry. "You don't know? Oh my goodness. How is it you don't know?"

Henry was confused, what was she talking about? "Know what?"

"Esther is dead, Henry. Augustus killed her three months after you left New York."

Henry sat staring at the woman who saved his life. "That's not funny, Hannah."

He watched as a tear rolled down her cheek. "No, it wasn't. He beat her to death and then fled west somewhere. Esther's gone, and he's out there somewhere never having paid for killing her."

Henry reached for Hannah and she moved close, he took her hand. "I'm sorry, I didn't know. I'm sorry I wasn't there, maybe I could have stopped him."

Hannah looked into his eyes and he saw her pain hidden deep inside. "No one could have saved her. She knew he was mean. She knew he would hurt her and she even knew he'd kill her one day, but she wouldn't leave him. Not even for you. She was convinced she loved him."

Henry started to pull her toward him to comfort her when there came a loud screech from the foot of the bed. "BWAAKK!" Then he had a face full of brown and black feathers and a burning sensation in his hand. He jerked his hand away and looked at the huge rooster standing on the bed between him and Hannah. "What is that?"

Hannah smiled. "This is Bob, he's my protector."

Henry's face scrunched up in a frown. "You have an attack chicken?"

Hannah picked up the big fowl and started stroking it. "Bob isn't a chicken, he's a rooster. His job is to keep me safe and, as you can see, he takes it very seriously."

"Why'd he attack me?"

"He thought you were trying to get too forward with me, Marshal. Let that be a warning to you."

Henry shook his head. "If he comes after me again he better be warned, he just might become dinner."

Hannah glared at him. "No one is eating Bob. It's time for your pain medicine and then you need to rest. This afternoon I'll need to change your dressing and make sure that wound is not getting infected."

She handed Henry a glass of water with some medicine she'd mixed in from a bottle. He drank it knowing it would do no good to fight with her. He was hurting anyway, and he was also tired and sleepy just from sitting up and eating and talking. Who knew a bullet could take so much out of a man? As he drifted off to sleep, two things were on his mind. Who had shot him in the back? The second was that Esther was dead and her killer was free. What, if anything, could he do about that?

HANNAH TURNED Henry on his side and pulled the bandage free of his stitches. She looked and felt, noting that it wasn't hot or putrid which she didn't expect, but fever would be the first sign of infection. She put a clean bandage on and then left the mostly asleep patient to himself. She smiled as she looked at Bob sitting on the bottom right bed post staring at Henry like he was daring the Marshal to move. Penny Ryder had a strange sense of humor leaving that feisty rooster to look after her, but she had to admit he was doing an admiral job; maybe too good. If Henry couldn't get close to her at all, how was she supposed to convince him that he wanted to marry her? Even though he hadn't come right out and said it, she knew he knew that was going to be the outcome of this snowstorm and his getting shot. He'd hinted at it by talking about her reputation. The only way to save that was for him to do the right thing and marry her. She knew for her that wasn't a hardship, she'd been in love with him from the first time her sister had brought him home with her. He'd sat and talked to her, one of only a few people who listened when she told them she was going to go to college and become a nurse. Others, including Esther, had laughed at her but not Henry; he'd looked her in the eye for a few minutes and then nodded just once. "Hannah Coppersmith, I think you can become whatever you set your mind to become." That was what he'd said and that was when she knew she was in love with him. The only other person who listened was her best friend's grandpa, Nugget Nate Ryder, Penny's famous husband. He'd even gone so far as telling her father that when she was ready, there was a fund set for her to go to nursing school.

Sure enough, when she applied she was told that all classes had been paid for in full, all she needed was to purchase the materials she'd need and pay for boarding. Her father had seen to it that those were covered, because Mr. Ryder had let him in on one of his lucrative business deals with the understanding that Hannah would be allowed to follow her dream. It was the only thing that had kept her from being married off to someone like Augustus Rayner.

However, she had never forgotten that the first person to believe in her dream was Henry Wheeler. When her sister had told her that she had accepted Rayner's proposal, Hannah had begged her sister to marry Henry instead. When Esther had laughed and said Henry was a poor choice for a husband, Hannah had gotten mad and told her sister if Esther didn't want him, she'd take him. Esther had laughed even harder at that. "Oh Hannah, you are such a silly little girl. Henry doesn't even know you exist. If you don't believe me I'll prove it. I'll ask him to dance with you tonight, and when he doesn't you'll see he isn't worth this crush you've built up in your head. He's just some shopkeeper's son, not our kind. He was good for a few laughs and some stolen kisses, not much of anything else."

Yet here he was, a United States Marshal investigating the man who had almost ruined Hannah and eight other women. While Esther's perfect husband of their status was a murderer and wife beater on the run. But still, did Hannah want to be married to someone who was still in love with her dead sister? His reaction to being told she was dead had proved he'd still had feelings for Esther, and the fact that when he first saw her while he was lying in the road he'd thought she'd come to rescue him. She was confused and if it wasn't for the waist deep snow, she'd get outside and try to figure out if she wanted Henry Wheeler knowing he loved another.

She opened the door and grabbed the shovel she kept on the small porch for hauling out the ashes from the fire place and stove, and immediately set to clearing a path to the small three stall lean-to that housed her mare, Henry's stallion, and the cow someone had given her for payment of her medical services. She needed to make sure they were fed, and milk the cow before it became over-full and pained. The hard work of shoveling and cleaning and caring for the animals would give her time away from her patient and his effect on her thoughts and feelings. At least until she had to return to the cabin and see his half naked physique again. Why did that stupid Bob have to stop her from being able to feel his strong arms around her and his chiseled chest against her? Darn Penny and her stupid chaperone rooster anyway.

4

A couple of hours later, Hannah was back in her cabin watching over her patient as she went about doing what she needed to. Remembering Penny had told her there would be no other emergencies for a few days; she set about putting her small cabin to rights. She often didn't have time to clean like she should between helping Doctor Thomas at his clinic and seeing to the women's health needs that popped up from time to time. Recently she'd been seeing a few of the new brides in town. The first was Beatrice Jameson who was surprised to find she was in the family way and a bit worried how she would handle two children under two. Hannah had assured her women had been doing so for much longer than they'd been born, and had made the young wife and mother promise to eat right and send for her at the first sign of trouble or labor pains.

Just a few weeks ago Marta Clark had come to see her worried she was sick. The young woman had also been surprised by her condition and worried about adding another child to her already large family. Hannah herself had been worried a bit about her with five other children and Royce to look after, and had taken it upon herself to go see Royce and ask him to arrange some help for his wife. She hadn't told him that his Marta was pregnant, but had told him she was working herself into exhaustion. She'd suggested that he find someone to help with some of the cooking and cleaning around their place for a while and give Marta a chance to rest. When Marta finally told him she was with child, he would understand better what Hannah had been trying to tell him without ruining the surprise. 'Course knowing that Royce's first wife had died in childbirth, he might be even more of a mess than normal. She'd have to remember to talk to Doctor Thomas about the Clarks next time she saw him.

She cleaned up the area where she had slept the night before, folding everything and placing it back on the shelf it had come from. She'd need it again tonight, but she wanted to clean the floor first since it had been almost two weeks since she'd last had a chance to do so. She grabbed a bucket full of snow to put on the stove to melt and heat as she quickly cut up the two rabbits one of the trappers had given her yesterday as payment for sewing up a wound he claimed to have gotten skinning a beaver. It looked more like something he got from a broken bottle down at the Golden Nugget but she didn't say so, just sewed it up and took his two rabbits. They'd make a good rabbit stew she and Henry could have both for lunch and supper. She got the stew on and figured they'd use the leftover biscuits from breakfast with lunch; she'd whip up a pan of cornbread to go with the same stew for dinner. She was just starting on scrubbing the floor when Henry start moaning. She walked over and made sure that he wasn't hurting, but it seemed his moans were more from a dream than from the gunshot wound to his back. He was mumbling about killers and rustlers and she figured it was something he'd encountered as a member of the Marshal service.

She wondered what had possessed the dapper young man she had known in New York to not only join the Marshal Service, but to leave New York. She knew he'd been heartbroken when her sister rejected him, but had it been so bad that he'd fled everyone and everything he'd ever known for a life of danger and getting shot at? She could see as she looked at his bare chest and back that he'd taken other wounds through the years working as a Deputy Marshal and now Marshal. There were several knife scars or cutting scars and at least two other bullets scars that she could see. The young man she'd known in New York was gentle and as refined as anyone of her family's social status, even if he was a step below them. Could her sister's rejection of him have changed him so much? Was he even the man she'd loved or thought she'd loved all these years. The young man who had seen her and encouraged her was the measure to which all men since had been found lacking, but was that measure false in itself? She didn't know, and she didn't know how to find out in the next six and a half days before the time was up and people found out she'd had him in her place for a week alone. Did she even want to know this Henry Wheeler whose dreams were filled with violence and pain?

How could she find out if she had to keep him on the laudanum for his pain so he'd rest and heal? Maybe she should try an even lighter dose watered down even more. She didn't want him in pain, but not sound asleep would be good. Besides, she knew the opium in the drug would help loosen his tongue and inhibitions so that maybe she could learn about who he'd become in the last five years. She needed him to see her for who she was and not what he remembered or through the lens of his desire for Esther. Yes, she'd halve his dose after lunch and hope he'd feel like talking to her.

HENRY WOKE to another wonderful smell, some kind of stew unless he was mistaken. He slowly looked around without trying to sit up. The pain from earlier was starting to come back. The medicine Hannah had given him, while it took away his pain, had caused him to have vivid dreams that mixed his past with the thought of losing her to villains from his past, including Rayner. Why he was worried about losing Hannah was something he didn't want to think about, but knew he needed to. After all, if and when it was found out they'd spent time alone in her cabin during this snowstorm and the time until it thawed enough he could travel, he'd have no choice but to marry her. He couldn't leave her with a damaged reputation with the likes of Archie Grady and his crew running around. She wouldn't be safe from advances that she didn't deserve, especially on top of the fact that she already had the tarnish of being one of the "missing" women. He looked at her on her hands and knees scrubbing the floor on the other side of the table. Her backside was to him and he closed his eyes trying to get his body under control after his eyes had locked on to her perfectly shaped derrière as it moved with every push and pull of her arms. Little Hannah Coppersmith had grown into a beautiful and desirable young lady. One that he'd be a fool to deny he wouldn't mind being married to. Before he could get himself under control completely, there was a cluck and then a sharp pain in his hand. That stupid rooster almost seemed to know what he was thinking. He sighed loudly so that Hannah would know he was awake before he spoke so as not to startle her. "Must you keep that rooster in the cabin?"

She stopped scrubbing and turned to look at him. Some of her hair had worked itself loose from the two braids and hung around her face in ringlets. Henry wanted nothing more than to twirl them around his fingers and pull her in for a kiss of those full and promising looking lips. "It's too cold and the snow too deep for Bob to stay outside right now. Besides, his job is to protect my virtue and he couldn't do that outside, could he?"

"What in the world makes you think you need your virtue protected from me, Miss Coppersmith? I can't even sit up on my own right now. Speaking of which, I'm going to need to get out of this bed and find a necessary, I'm sorry to say."

Hannah sighed and placed her scrub brush in the bucket sitting beside her. "I'll help you get upright and get you the chamber pot. Then I'll go out and check on your horse and mine. Please don't do yourself damage while I'm gone."

She stood and walked over, reaching under the bed and pulling out a chamber pot and setting it on a chair she put beside the bed. She helped Henry sit up for a few minutes to get his pain and weakness under control and then helped him stand. He shook like a newborn colt. She looked up at him, "Are you going to be okay if I leave, or should I just turn around facing the other way and help hold you up?"

Henry turned red. He wanted to tell her to leave but he knew, as embarrassing as it would be to have her hold him up while he emptied his bladder, if she let him go now he was going to fall and embarrass himself even more. As sweat popped out on his forehead she nodded without him saying anything, and slowly turned so she faced the bed and held on to him with both arms, her head buried in his back to give him as much privacy and stability as she could.

He wanted to curse, but knew it would just embarrass them both more. So he quickly undid his buttons and took care of the matter at hand. Once he was finished she helped him sit down; he lay down totally worn out. "Why am I so weak? It's not like this is the first time I've been shot. I don't remember being this weak the last time."

Hannah took the chamber pot out and returned quickly, letting in a blast of cold air that had them both shivering and Bob's feathers puffing. She put the pot back under the bed and sat in the chair facing him. "I told you this morning you lost a lot of blood. That's why you are so weak. It wasn't the bullet itself that has done you in, but the loss of blood and laying on the frozen ground for who knows how long before I found you. If you keep resting and eating what I give you, then in a few days, you should be feeling more like your old self, strength and energy wise. It will take a while longer for the bullet wound to heal, but the fact that it missed your spine is a good thing, Henry. You could have been paralyzed if it had been a half inch more to the left. Or collapsed a lung, an inch more to the right. As it was, it just damaged some muscle that I'm sure you'll recover once you're mended."

"I know you're right, but that doesn't help me right now. I need to figure out who shot me and if Reverend Theodore survived his near hanging. Plus, now I have to worry about harming your reputation, too."

"Henry, you can't do anything about any of those things right now. For now, you need to concentrate on getting well. We'll worry about repercussions when we must, but until then rest, heal, and let's get reacquainted; we both know what will be expected of us when word gets out. I'd rather at least be friends again before that happens."

Henry saw the truth of her statement in her face. She, like him, knew they'd have no choice but to marry to save her from ruin, and she was right; they needed to become reacquainted before that happened. She obviously wasn't the little wallflower he'd last seen in New York any more than he was the future shopkeeper she'd known. Life and time had changed them both. Her into a beautiful woman who had fulfilled her dream of becoming a nurse. Him, well he was a man still lost in the numbness he'd built around himself at her sister's rejection. Hannah deserved better than him. He didn't know how he could let down his walls to become what she deserved, but he'd have to try because she deserved his heart if he could find it.

5

That night after supper Hannah checked Henry's wound again. Still it was clean, dry, and seemed to have no infection. After lunch she had washed most of the blood out of the shirt she'd cut off him. Now she tried to sew it back together if for no other reason than so he wouldn't be half-dressed when someone came to visit when the week was over. It was hard to sit and sew and talk to Henry. His chest and stomach kept distracting her. She found herself wondering how the hair on his chest and stomach would feel under her hands. Would it be soft and downy like those on some of the babies she'd delivered, or wiry and rough like the rest of him? She blushed at the direction her thoughts were taking her. Henry didn't feel about her like she did him. He'd only agreed they get to know each other again because they both knew that they were going to be forced to marry when word of his staying with her got out. Otherwise, Hannah would become a target for every unscrupulous womanizer in Creede and Creede was full of men of that type. She'd do well to keep her thoughts on that fact, too instead of fantasizing about the man who still loved her sister.

She turned her mind to fixing his shirt. "Why did you rip my coat and shirt off? Why not just remove them before you got me in the bed?"

She looked at him. "How strong do you think I am, Henry Wheeler? It took everything I had just to get you here and in that bed. You were almost dead; I didn't have time to worry about your clothes. I can fix the shirt and I'll have Doctor Thomas or one of the Reverends get you a new coat as soon as I can. You should be thankful I could get you here at all; you weigh almost twice what I do, you know."

She watched as awareness of how difficult it would have been for her dawned on him and she felt a bit guilty. After all, she had Heavenly help and probably could have gotten the coat and shirt off without cutting it but she wasn't thinking just reacting.

"You're right, Hannah. I'm sorry; it's just embarrassing to lay here half-naked in front of you. I am grateful for what you did for me. Seems to me that I was right all those years ago when I told you I thought you'd make a good nurse. You are a good nurse, maybe better than a good nurse. I'm not sure Doc Thomas could have fixed me any better than you did."

She smiled. "I'm surprised you remember that conversation, Henry, it was so long ago."

"He looked at her, "Of course I remember it. You were so determined even then. I could see it in your eyes. I knew you would make it because I could see you weren't going to let anyone or anything tell you that you couldn't. I even told Esther to stop teasing you about it. I know she didn't but I told her she should encourage you to go for your dreams. I'm alive right now because you did. So thank you."

He held out his hand to her and she set his shirt on her lap and took his hand in hers. He looked into her eyes; it was as if something sparked to life between them. He raised her hand toward his lips and was about to kiss her fingers when suddenly Bob was clucking and flying around his head pecking and pulling at his hair. He dropped her hand to try and grab the rooster but all he got was a handful of pin feathers as the poultry protector hopped away.

Hannah covered her mouth to keep from laughing out loud as Henry swore up a blue streak at the rooster who was once again sitting at the foot of the bed watching over them.

"Seriously, Hannah, you need to cook that bird. He's about the most evil thing I've ever seen."

"He's doing his job, Henry. Keeping me safe and my virtue intact."

Henry glared at the bird. "I don't see why that matters seeing as how everyone will believe what they want when we're discovered anyway."

She stilled and glared at him. "Maybe so, Marshal Wheeler, but we'll know the truth. I've survived to the age of twenty-three, gone through nursing school, traveled three-quarters of the way across the country, kidnapped, freed, and worked as a nurse all without losing my virtue. I will not lose it to the likes of you just because we both know we'll have to wed. I will come to our marriage bed pure or not at all."

Henry held up his hands as if afraid either she or Bob would lay into him again. "I didn't mean to upset you Hannah, or imply that I didn't think you were pure or virtuous. Maybe you should just give me another dose of that pain medicine and let me go back to sleep. After all, you did tell me to rest."

Hannah sighed and shook her head. "I'm sorry; I guess

I'm just getting stressed with all this, too. It is too early to give you another dose of medication. This stuff is very dangerous; people get to where they need it even when not sick or in pain so I'm very cautious about using it. I'll make your next dose a bit stronger so it gets you through the night but for now, just talk to me. Tell me how you ended up a U.S. Marshal. I mean, the last time I saw you was when my sister got engaged and you had planned on taking over for your father at the shop."

He looked at her and then nodded like he'd made a decision to share. "That was the night I decided to become a member of the Marshal service. I left the party upset. I had asked your sister to marry me that night, too. Only she told me Augustus asked her earlier and she'd said yes. I was hurt and shocked; I didn't even know she was seeing him. He used to brag about the things his society girl would do for him that even the girls at the gentlemen's clubs wouldn't. All that time I had no idea he was talking about Esther. I left and grew angry the closer to home I got. Then I saw a billboard flyer on a post about joining the Marshal Service and living a life of adventure. I guess I got pretty drunk, but when I woke up the next day all I could think about was running the shop and having to see your sister when she'd come in to buy things. I couldn't do that so I went and signed up. I worked in the Wall Street office for a year. Mostly as office staff and jailer. Then a Deputy from New Mexico Territory walked in hauling Elizabeth Ryder's husband in cuffs. He'd gone after Elizabeth with a buggy whip and when the Marshal tried to stop him, he attacked the Marshal. Turned out Reverend Ryder had gone to New Mexico Territory for his health and sent the deputy back to bring his daughter and her children to him after her divorce. Her husband was also beating her and stealing her inheritance. The deputy asked me to travel with him; seemed they needed more lawmen to deal with a situation. So I thought if I left the state, maybe I could move on with my life. I did but I didn't. Now I'm here and you're here and well, I reckon we'll make the best of the situation."

Hannah nodded. "Yes, I guess we will. But Henry, I want to ask you to take your time and find a way to let my sister go. I may end up having to be married to you, but I don't want to be a substitute for Esther."

She got up and looked back at the man in her bed as she put on her coat and scarf. "I need to go milk the cow and check on our horses. I'll give you your medicine when I get back. She left before he could see the tears in her eyes. Tears for him and his hardened heart, tears for her and her shattered one.

HENRY WATCHED as Hannah left to check on the livestock. He wasn't fooled; he'd seen the tears in her eyes. He didn't know how to tell her that she would never be a substitute for her sister. What he thought he'd felt for Esther wasn't anything. Yes, in his near death he'd thought Hannah was Esther for a moment, but how could he let Hannah know she was even lovelier than her sister had ever been. Just her zeal for her work made her more appealing. Her bravery made her more appealing. She'd left everyone she'd ever known to come west, and for what? To answer the call of a doctor who needed help caring for the sick and injured of this town. Even after she was kidnapped and held against her will, almost sold into a life of whoring, she still stayed right here in Creede and started taking care of the medical needs of its citizens. Even in his situation, she could have left him to die or taken the safer route and gotten him to the Doctor's clinic even if it had meant his death. But knowing what it would mean she'd brought him here to her home and cared for him. Now she was not only tending his wound but cooking, cleaning, and mending for him as if he were already her husband.

No, he wouldn't say she was a substitute for her sister in his mind. She was something so much more. But could he love her? Oh, he was attracted to her. She was beautiful and he wanted to see that gorgeous hair loose and flowing around her. He wanted to run his fingers through it and pull her into his arms and taste her and hold her. But did he love her? He didn't know. Five years ago he'd locked up his heart and promised to never use it again and until this day, he'd never even wanted to. Oh, he wasn't pure; he'd been to Big Bertha's more than a few times back in Redemption. Not that he made a big deal about it but he'd had his share of women. It was the one point of contention he and Nathan had always had. But his heart was never involved in any of those transactions.

He couldn't get the thought of Hannah's tears out of his mind. He didn't know if love was possible for him, but for this amazing woman he'd try and find a way to unlock his heart. Until then, maybe it was best if that stupid rooster stayed perched on the foot of the bed to keep him honest.

When she opened the door and returned, he could see and hear the wind howling down the valley. Snowdrifts were blowing around. Already it felt colder than it had when she had gone out to check on the animals. She carried in a bucket of milk and sat it on the dry sink to settle before she strained it.

"Sounds and feels like the temperature is going to drop, thanks to the wind blowing through. Maybe you should think about bundling under the covers with me tonight so you don't freeze on the floor."

Hannah's head snapped around to him. "I don't think that's a good idea. First, the chance of accidentally hurting you is too great; and secondly, I will be perfectly fine in my nest of furs and quilts. I have an abundance of them as payment for my services to the trappers and miners wives."

"Well, what about me? I don't think it would be good for me to get cold in my weakened condition."

"I can spare a few furs for you, too, and if you want something warm and soft to cuddle and share heat with, then snuggle up with Bob. She picked up the rooster and sat him on Henry's chest. "He's warm and with all those feathers it will be like having a down comforter next to you."

The blasted poultry moved off his chest and nested down against his left side, clucking softly and preening just like he understood what Hannah had said. Henry wanted to toss the fowl aside but he wasn't about to give Hannah the satisfaction of knowing she'd gotten the better of him. "Yes, that will do quite well. Bob snores less than you do anyway."

He swallowed his laughter as Hannah rounded on him. "I will have you know, Henry Wheeler, that I do not snore!"

"How do you know you don't since you're asleep when it happens?"

Her mouth opened and shut several times before she turned around and pulled the glass bottle and spoon off the shelf and quickly stirred a dose of the medicine into a glass of water. "Take your medicine before I decide not to give you any and let you suffer for that remark."

He grinned and struggled to sit enough to drink down the potion she'd made. Then he lifted a hand and stroked her check. "I'm teasing, Hannah, and I want you to know I'd never see you as a substitute for Esther; she was tin plating next to the silver you are."

He laid back and let the warmth of the opium in the medicine take him deep into healing sleep. Never seeing Hannah's hand come up and rest where he'd stroked her face.

6

Henry looked around and slowly sat up. He was a bit stronger today but the pain was also a bit worse. Hannah was nowhere to be seen and neither was that pesky rooster, which meant she'd probably gone out to the barn again. He wondered how it was going to work once they were married. Yes, she lived in this little line shack halfway between Topaz and Creede, but his office was in Topaz and he had a small apartment that was honestly a bit bigger than her place here. His barn was also larger because Nathan had paid to have it built to hold a string of horses in case he needed to deputize a posse or had need of a bigger string of mounts for himself. So on one hand it would make sense for them to live in Topaz. But if Hannah was going to continue to work for Doctor Thomas, that would be a long ride for her and he wasn't sure he wanted her making it every day.

'Course they weren't married yet and while he was fairly positive that they would end up married at the end of this storm, there really wasn't a guarantee that would happen. He wouldn't let her reputation be destroyed or leave her at the mercy of Archie or the more unscrupulous men in and around the area. However, he knew she didn't want to marry him. Her words last night kept coming to his mind. He couldn't understand what had made her tell him she wouldn't be a substitute for her sister. Even if Esther were alive and able to marry him there was no possible scenario he could think of that would have him standing at the altar with her. His love for her had quickly faded after her declaration that he was just a plaything while she'd waited for what she really wanted. He couldn't see Hannah ever toying with someone's affection like that. Everything about Hannah appealed to him. Her beauty, she'd been a pretty girl but she was a beautiful woman. Every curve she had called to him and the thought of her on her hands and knees scrubbing the floor yesterday still left him besotted. But it was more than her looks. After he realized who she was, he'd watched her without being obvious about it. He'd seen how she treated everyone with kindness and respect. The soiled doves she treated for womanly issues, the wives of both the citizens of Creede and the miners' families as well. Everyone, even the smelliest and meanest of the miners themselves she treated with kindness and compassion. The only person he'd ever seen her treat badly was Archie Grady, and seeing as how everyone knew he was behind the snatching of the women, he didn't blame her.

But how could he go about convincing her of that? While he'd never planned to marry and start a family after leaving New York, the thought wasn't unpleasant to him anymore. As a matter of fact, if the woman he married was Hannah, the thought was more than pleasant; it was almost desirable. Was it love? Probably not, he didn't think he had enough of a heart left to ever love again. But it was something. Like an itch one needed to scratch but couldn't quite reach.

The door opened and in came Hannah, a bucket of milk in each hand. "Good morning, Henry. How are you feeling this morning? In pain?"

"Some, but mostly thoughtful. Something you said last night won't leave me alone."

She sat the buckets on the counter by the dry sink. "Oh?"

Henry struggled to his feet and walked over to where she stood. "You told me you wouldn't be a substitute for your sister." He shook his head. "I have never even thought of you as a replacement for Esther."

She looked down; he reached out and lifted her head by the chin so that she was looking into his eyes. "Understand this, Hannah Coppersmith. Whatever love you think I harbor for Esther died five years ago when she told me how I was just an amusement for her while she waited on Rayner. Yes, I left New York so that I wouldn't have to see them. More so that I wouldn't harbor anger and end up doing something I'd regret out of unrequited love. I may not love you, Hannah, but I do know that you are a woman worth having.

"You're kind and compassionate, not to mention beautiful and very desirable. I think maybe it's a good thing Bob is around to protect you."

At his name the feathered beast clucked and then crowed as if to remind Henry he was indeed there to protect Hannah. She blushed and then shook her head. "Those feelings of desire, Henry, they aren't real. It's the medicine, not how you really feel."

He frowned "What are you talking about?"

She held up the clear glass bottle half-full of a brownish

colored liquid. "This is laudanum; it's a mixture of opium and alcohol. It tends to make one a bit, shall we say amorous as well as lower their inhibitions and take away their pain. It's why it's so popular around the saloon girls. They take it and care a little less about what their jobs are. Unfortunately, it takes more to do the same thing the longer they take it until they can't live without it."

Henry looked from the bottle to her. "You think the way I feel about you comes out of that little bottle? You're saying I find you attractive and desirable because you've been giving me that medicine?"

She nodded as a tear rolled down her face. "Yes, that's exactly what I'm saying."

He looked at her for a minute before he looked at Bob. "I'm going to kiss her now, Bob, to prove a point. Please don't attack me."

The rooster let out a loud "Brawlk" and turned his back on them as if giving his permission. Henry brought his hands up and placed them on either side of her face. He leaned down and brought his lips to hers, gently at first, and then as the spark of his desire caught flame, with a bit more passion. When he heard the rooster starting to move around he gentled the kiss and ended it. "Does that seem to you to be coming from some medicine I've taken? How long do those effects last anyway? I know the pain control has worn out already; does the amorous desire last longer than the pain numbing?"

She looked into his eyes "No, it all wears off in about four to six hours."

He stroked her cheek with the back of his right hand. "How long would you say it's been since I had any of this magic medicine, then?"

"About eight hours."

"Then I think it's safe to say, Hannah Coppersmith, that my affection and desire for you are my own and not something out of that bottle."

She blushed and pulled away from his hand. "Do you need a dose for the pain?"

Henry looked at her rosy cheeks and thought about it. He wanted to keep flirting and sparking as much as her feathered protector would allow, but he wanted her to be positive that the desire was his, not the medicine. "Do you have something else I can take for the pain?"

She thought for a minute. "I could make you some willow bark tea. It's not as strong but it should help some with the pain."

"Then how about I have that till after dinner unless the pain gets worse. I also would like to be able to go to the necessary instead of using that chamber pot, and I think a lighter pain medicine would help with that."

Hannah nodded and then went and scooped some snow into a kettle and placed it on the stove. "I'll make you the tea and some breakfast. After that, I'll go clear a better path to the privy. Until then you use the chamber pot and rest. You're stronger than yesterday but you are still weaker than you were before you got shot."

She walked close; he reached out and pulled her into his arms and kissed her again. He was getting good and lost in her scent and the feel of her in his arms when there came a series of rooster squawks and a sharp pain in his big toe where the evil rooster had pecked him. "Wow, Bob, you just wait till I'm my healed self. I'll pluck ya alive for that."

The bird puffed himself up to his larger than average size, looked Henry in the eye from a sideways cocked head, and then let him know exactly what he thought of Henry's threat with a furious flapping of wings and a hearty "COCK-A-DOODLE-DOO."

Hannah started giggling as she spun away and started on a breakfast of pancakes and home fries with several strips of bacon thrown in for extra energy. Henry hobbled back to the bed and put on his mended denim shirt before settling into the chair that still sat beside Hannah's bed he'd slept in for the last two days. "Tonight, Hannah, you take the bed. I'll bed down in the nest on the floor."

She opened her mouth like she was going to complain. "I'll nap in the bed this afternoon, but I won't keep your bed from you. Either we find a way to share it so you're comfortable, or I'll sleep on the floor."

Hannah gave a quick nod and went back to cooking. Henry settled and couldn't keep his eyes off of her. She even looked lovely being domestic. Yep, he was taking her straight to the preacher as soon as they could get down the trail. No two ways about it.

∼

Hannah went back to cooking as if she hadn't heard the last few sentences that Henry had said. Her lips still tingled with the two soul searing kisses he'd given her. Her first two from someone that wasn't related to her. Oh, guys had tried but she'd never allowed it before. But Henry's kisses had been perfect. Her heart had started hammering when he told Bob he was going to kiss her and when he did she thought she'd die from the sheer wonderful feelings of his warm firm lips against hers. When he'd pressed in letting her feel the passion he was keeping tight control over, she thought she'd combust from the heat and tingle of it. The second unexpected one had literally turned her legs to water and if he hadn't been holding her she'd have melted into a puddle of melted nurse right at his feet.

But it was the words as he'd sat beside the bed that wouldn't let her go. He'd made it plain they'd share the bed tonight or he'd sleep on the floor. She couldn't let him take the floor; it would be detrimental to his recovery and healing. But the thought of lying next to him... well, if she was honest, it thrilled her in a way that she knew a good and proper Christian girl shouldn't be thrilled. But the part of her that knew they would end up married at the end of their exile really wanted to know what it would feel like to lay next to him with his strong arms holding her. Was it wrong? She knew society and her mother would say yes but if they were just sleeping, sharing heat, was it? It wasn't like he wasn't going to be forced to marry her anyway. What was a couple of nights being held and holding the man she wanted more than any other? Would Bob allow it? If he did, should she? She turned her mind back to the task at hand as the kettle began to whistle. She quickly pulled it off the stove and poured the water into the cup with the willow bark in it. She'd steep it while she finished the breakfast and then strain it and give it to Henry. It wouldn't take away the pain like the laudanum would, but since he insisted he wanted to spend time with her without the drug's amorous effects, she would give him the tea. If she saw the pain was too much, he'd take the drug or she'd sic that rooster on him till he gave in. But if drinking the tea would let him kiss her again like the last kiss, she'd let him slide for now.

She set the table and watched as he drank down the tea and refilled his cup with coffee, knowing he'd want it with breakfast. As they started to eat, Henry took the conversation in a new direction. "So I'm not going to pretend I don't know what will happen when we can get out of here,

Hannah. We both know we'll marry; sometime this week when I'm sure you know I am not marrying you as a replacement for Esther, I'll ask you properly to be my wife. However, we do need to talk a little about where we'll live and stuff."

Hannah looked at him. "What do you mean?"

"I mean I know you will want to keep working as a nurse and midwife and, honestly, since I'm one of the people who told you to not give up on that dream, I want you to keep working. I also know I'm the U.S. Marshal in these parts. You work with Doctor Thomas on the other side of Creede and my office is in Topaz. You have this place and I have a place over the Marshal's office and jail in Topaz. We need to figure out where to live and how to make it work for whichever one of us moves."

Hannah stopped. It wasn't the logistics of it all that shocked her but the fact that obviously Henry had been thinking about them. Less than an hour earlier, she'd accused him of being interested in her because of his pain medication, while he was thinking about how to combine their two lives together as husband and wife. That, more than the kisses, more than the promise that he didn't care for her sister anymore, his careful thought of how to mesh their individual lives and passions together convinced her he really didn't mind that they were going to be joined in marriage.

"What answers have you come up with?"

He sighed. "I haven't. If we live here, I'll have days that I'll have no choice but to leave you alone when I have prisoners or if my duties require I stay in Topaz. The fact that they don't have another lawman right now is also a concern for me. They aren't as big or as lawless as Creede but it wouldn't take much for the small saloon to become a powder keg.

"I also don't like the idea of moving you to Topaz. While my space is bigger and has a private bedroom, it means you'll have to travel twice as far to help out at the clinic and I don't like that idea, either."

"Yes, I can see your concerns. However, I don't really have to go to the doctor's clinic every day. A lot of times I could just go see a woman at her place. Plus, if I remember, there isn't a doctor in Topaz, either, is there?"

Henry shook his head. "No, closest thing is the barber and he's more of a leecher and stitcher than anything like a doctor."

"Topaz has a telegraph office, right?"

"I don't know but I have a set up in the Marshal's office for official business."

"So if someone really needed me they could send a wire, correct?"

"I'm sure we could come up with an arrangement with Mr. Jameson. What are you thinking?"

"If you have more room and there is a need for medical services, maybe I could move to Topaz and only have to come to Creede or Bachelor for a delivery or to deal with the girls at the saloons once in a while."

Hannah watched as Henry's fork stopped halfway to his mouth. "What do you mean, the girls at the saloons?"

"That's part of what I do for Doctor Thomas. I deal with the doves when they need doctoring of the womanly kind."

"I didn't realize that was a large part of what you do. I mean, I've seen you be nice to them in town but I didn't realize you were doctoring them."

She looked at him. "Henry, someone has to make sure

they are okay and not sickly. It's better for them if it's me, better for Doctor Thomas, too. He's single, you know."

"Never thought about it. Don't know if I like that, Hannah."

"You don't have to like it but I won't stop helping them when they need it. Unless it's an emergency, we could schedule those trips and you could go with me. You couldn't be in the room with me but you could wait out on the landing."

Henry thought about it and finally she saw him nod as he agreed. "You're right. I just said I didn't want to stop you from doing what you felt led to do. I'll not be making myself a liar now. I do like the idea of coming with you and if there's an emergency and I'm near, I would like to be there then, too. I think if Doctor Thomas is agreed, we have a good plan. Are you going to be all right coming to live in Topaz with me?"

"As long as Bob and Hazel can come with me."

Henry frowned. "Who is Hazel?"

"My cow."

"Oh well then I have no problem with the cow; she can stay in the barn behind the Marshal's office. But the rooster... I don't want him living with us after we're married."

She hid her smile. "Bob is just doing his job, Henry. I'm sure after we're married he'll be more than happy to look for his own hens and roost."

"Well, you just make sure he knows I won't put up with him attacking me for sparking with my wife."

The bird looked at him and hopped up on her lap before crowing long and loud as if to say, "She ain't yours yet, boy."

7

Henry hurt; his back felt like it had been... well, like it had been shot, which it had and only two days ago. But the snow and wind had finally died down and he figured if it warmed up a bit in a few days the trail would be passable and they'd either get some company or they'd ride into Creede and check on Reverend Eugene and have him perform their wedding. Henry hadn't gotten to steal but a couple more kisses before that stupid rooster started making such a racket they couldn't stay together. He was either pecking at Henry's feet, or he'd jump and kick those wicked spurs at his chest or side, trying to scratch the Marshal, or he'd put extra effort into it and end up flapping his wings at Henry's head and trying to peck at the top of his hair yanking it. Finally, Hannah had declared she needed to go clear the path to the privy anyway, and took the cantankerous fowl with her.

Henry wished he wasn't weak and didn't have a hole in his back; he'd be the one shoveling the path instead of sitting here while Hannah did it. Of course, if he hadn't been shot and lost so much blood, he wouldn't be here at all.

While he didn't enjoy being shot in the back by some low-down, yellow-bellied pole cat, he couldn't be too upset because it brought him an unexpected jewel in the form of Hannah Coppersmith. Now he was going to be married to her, something that might never have happened if not for the shooter. That got him thinking about two things. The first, who did shoot him? His first thought was that Ketchem had tried to kill him before his investigation could prove the sheriff was as crooked as that tree rumor said Mrs. Fontaine had fled to when she killed that cougar. However, the man had yelped in surprise and returned fire so that didn't seem likely. But he hadn't heard anyone else ride up behind him. Maybe the yelp wasn't surprise at being shot at as much as the fact that Henry hadn't dropped dead right then. Henry wasn't sure if he'd ever be able to find the person that shot him unless they tried again, but he learned a valuable lesson: never leave his back open to anyone he didn't trust beyond a shadow of a doubt. Nathan had told him that a thousand times, but he'd gotten complacent riding with the infamous Preacher.

The other thought was he hadn't taken care of his gun since that night when he fired it to drop Eugene out of that noose. He reached over to the post at the head of the bed, pulled both Peacemakers out of the holster, and unloaded them. He pulled a cleaning kit out of his saddle bag that Hannah had placed under the head of the bed. He cleaned and oiled both six shooters and reloaded them. He'd only fired the one round that night. Never even saw who put a slug in his back. He wondered if Hannah had kept the bullet. That might be a useful thing to have. It would at least tell him what kind of weapon he'd been shot with. He also needed her to bring him his rifle. While he hadn't fired it, he had pulled it from the saddle boot and exposed it to the elements. At the least, he needed to make sure it was dry and well-oiled so it would be in good working order when he could use it again. If his coat wasn't ruined he'd try and get in some practice while snowed in. He could pick a target behind the line shack even if he just tossed a couple of those empty fruit tins out to shoot at.

That was another thing he'd learned from Nathan. Practice every day. Both speed and, more importantly, accuracy. It had paid off when he'd needed to be accurate to save Eugene's neck, literally. He remembered how hard Nathan had to work after his return to Redemption from Cottonwood. He, too, had been shot in the back on the same side if he remembered correctly, and it had taken Nathan months of daily target and quick draw practice to get back where he was before the shooting. Nathan still claimed he was slower than before he was shot but no one else saw that. Henry hadn't shot either his Colts or his Henry for two days now. And while that wasn't enough to get rusty, the weakness and pull of the stitches did concern him. What if he ended up needing his skills to protect himself or, worse, Hannah? He lifted both pistols only to have them start to shake badly before he even got them to firing height.

He stood and strapped the gun belt to his waist, got it set and tried a right-hand draw, and gasped before his hand even reached the six-gun in his holster. Lifting it with any speed was not going to happen. He tried the left and while he could get the gun out, he had no real control over the pistol and the pain was almost as bad as the right hand. He got set to try drawing left handed again when the door opened and Hannah came in. She stopped and her eyes got wide. "What do you think you're doing, Henry Wheeler?"

"I'm testing my draw, Hannah. It's a necessary skill in my line of work."

"Are you trying to undo all my hard work? You'll rip the stitches doing that this soon. Take that belt off and get back in the bed."

"You don't understand."

She rushed over and tugged the belt loose from his waist. "No, you don't understand. I'm going to say it one more time, Henry. YOU... ALMOST... DIED. You lost a lot of blood and it took a lot of stitches to close the hole blown in your back. Now take that shirt off and turn around; I need to see if you ripped the stitches loose."

She reached for the buttons on his shirt and had it off before he could tease her about undressing him. Then she was behind him poking and prodding at the area where he'd been shot. "Good, you didn't tear anything loose. No more trying to use these until the stitches come out."

"You don't understand."

"I do understand. I get how important these weapons are to your job, but you will not undo all my hard work and risk getting an infection and dying before we are married. I won't allow that, Henry. A couple of weeks won't hurt you that much. It will give you time to build your strength back up, too."

He sighed; he knew when he'd been beat. That was another thing he'd learned from watching the Ryders. When a woman was not going to budge on something she said. He saw the same fire and determination in her eyes that Grace, Elizabeth, and Rebecca Ryder had on occasions with their men. Never once had he seen Nathan, Rowdy, or even David win when that look was used. So, he just nodded and put the gun-belt back on the bedpost.

∼

HANNAH AND HENRY talked as they ate, and she continued to work around the cabin. It was hard to get too excited about some of the cleaning jobs she needed to do because of the talk they'd had about her moving to Topaz with him after the wedding. But she wanted to leave the place in better shape for Waylon's men than it had been when he'd offered to rent it to her. She would get it cleaned, and when the time came to leave, she would make sure it was fully stocked with beans and flour and other staples like coffee and cornmeal, some tins of peaches and dried apples. She'd have Henry lay in fire wood, and she'd make sure all the original bed covers were clean and pressed. This would give her something to do while she and Henry were stuck here alone together.

While he was awake and willing to talk, they did. They talked about their lives before they came to Creede and learned about the adult versions of each other. Hannah heard of the things Henry had helped Marshal Ryder and Marshal Cody with in and around Redemption and the New Mexico territory. She talked about nursing school and her mother trying to force her to become a proper society lady after her sister's death. She explained the deal Nugget Nate had made her father and that, for the first time she could ever remember, her father had gone against her mother's wishes and insisted Hannah finish her training and even agreed that she should look for a nursing position.

Henry talked about learning to live, not only as a lawman, but how to be a good one in the wild western territories. It was different than what he'd learned in New York as a Marshal. Back east people had respect for the badge; in the west they either feared it or belittled it, unless you could back it up with justice and a quick, accurate gun. While he was no shootist like Nathan Ryder or Bart Cody, he wasn't slow and could hit what he aimed at with either hand and with a rifle.

He explained how Nathan had made him practice every day, not just with pistol and rifle, but with knife and whip and even bow and arrow. Henry knew that Nathan held the same belief that Nugget Nate had: A man learned to use whatever weapon was at hand. On top of that, he learned how to read people, how to spot trouble before it happened, how to stop trouble before it happened or to end it once it had. To bring justice or even vengeance. Hannah was amazed at the change in him. He told her himself and his stories proved it; he left New York City a boy, but had become a man in New Mexico. Now he was about to become her man in just a few short days. Just as soon as they could travel up the trail.

With dinner, talk turned to Henry's declaration that she would either share the bed with him that night, or have it to herself. "Henry, you won't heal sleeping on the floor. You need to stay in the bed so that your back is protected from the hardness of the floor."

"Then we need to figure out how we will both sleep in the bed, Hannah, because I can see you aren't getting enough rest on the floor. You are starting to look tired and worn out, and I won't have it. You want me to rest and heal, but I won't be able to if you end up exhausted and sick. So, what can we do?"

The bed wasn't super narrow like a lot of line shacks were. Being closer to the main trail between Topaz and Creede, this one had been equipped for use by travelers who might need to get out of the weather as well as ranch hands. The bed was large enough for two, but how could they both sleep in it without violating their convictions? Well, her convictions. She wasn't so sure that Henry would be as concerned with her coming to their marriage bed pure. But she was not just concerned, but determined.

"If we were in New York or even some of the boarding houses along the way west there would be a bundling board, but we don't have anything like that."

"No, we don't. Maybe we could use some of those extra quilts and furs you were talking about."

"How do you mean?"

Henry smiled and took her hand. "You could get under all the covers, and I could lay on top of what's there now and cover with a quilt or fur or two. We could also roll a couple to place between us."

Hannah thought about that for a minute and then nodded. "That could work. And if I know Bob, he'll be right there keeping watch over us."

Henry nodded. "I just want to say again, after we are married that rooster will not be living inside with us. I'll get you some hens and build a coop next to the barn, but I won't have that beast interfering with us after we've pledged ourselves to each other."

Hannah blushed and smiled. "His job was to protect me and my virtue. I'm sure he'll be just fine with giving the job to you as my husband."

Henry looked down at the bird who was sitting on the far end of the table watching and listening. "I don't care if he likes it or not. I'll be doing the job after our I do's are said."

After dinner was eaten and the dishes cleaned, Hannah helped Henry back to the bed. She rolled two quilts together and placed them down the middle of the bed, and insisted that Henry get under the original sheets since she had a few more things to do and one of them was give him a dose of laudanum. He started to resist until she told him that if they were going to share the bed, he would need the extra pain relief as every move she made would cause him pain without it. He agreed and soon was fast asleep. After changing into her flannel nightgown, and stoking the fireplace, and banking the kitchen stove, Hannah climbed in the bed on the far side and settled into the covers. Just before she slipped off to sleep, she felt a weight on the quilts between her and Henry. She looked to see Bob nesting between them, helping to keep a level of separation. Hannah smiled, knowing that Henry was right; the rooster would have to stay outside after their wedding. But for now, he was doing the job her guardian angel had given him; protecting her virtue.

8

Their time had flown. After their first night sharing the bed, they had agreed the plan worked; by the sixth day alone in Hannah's cabin they had mostly fallen into a routine. Henry was getting around better and had gained much of his strength back. He was even going out to the lean-to barn with Hannah when she milked the cow and fed the horses. His stallion, Fury, was getting as antsy as Henry; both felt trapped here without being able to get out. He needed to be searching for the man who shot him in the back. Hannah had saved the bullet; he could tell it was a small caliber round from a small pocket gun or derringer. He was even more sure that Ketchem had tried to kill him. But why the deception? Why not just pull his Peacemaker and finish what he'd started? He could have let the Reverend hang and his boss would have been happy. Two problems removed at once. Henry never understood the working of the outlaw's mind. But he wondered how Ketchem would react when the weather allowed Henry to ride into Creede again. Henry found he was looking forward to it.

While Hannah wouldn't let him draw or fire his Colts or his rifle, he had begun lifting them over and over to help build his muscles. Nothing fast or fancy, just lifting them to shoulder height and lowering them slowly again and again to build his strength. As soon as Hannah or Doc took out the stitches, he'd be back out practicing every day till his speed and accuracy returned.

Each morning after they woke, Henry would pull Hannah into his arms and kiss her until that dadblamed rooster would peck or flap at him. Each day he was becoming more enamored of the woman she'd become; it became harder not to pull her into that bed without the extra covers separating them and show her just how much she was coming to mean to him. Yet there was still enough of the gentleman he'd been raised to be to refrain. The kisses were growing longer and more passionate and he fought to keep his hands on her hips or the back of her head and neck. She came away from them breathless and, more often than not, a bit shaky as well. Henry finally admitted to himself this sixth day of their time together that he couldn't think of what his life would be like without her in it. He didn't want to contemplate what it would be like not to see her face first thing in the morning or last thing before falling asleep. That afternoon as she sat across the table from him at lunch he came to realize that his heart beat faster when he caught her looking at him. That without trying he could tell where she was in the room. He wondered if that would hold true once they could leave this little cabin. He was almost startled by the realization that he was in love with Hannah Coppersmith. Henry Wheeler who had locked his heart away and promised himself he'd never love again, had gone and fallen in love with the woman he was going to have to marry. Only now he wanted to marry her. It wasn't so much he had to for her sake, but that he had to so that he wouldn't lose her in a town filled with single men.

When it came time to turn in for the night and she offered him a dose of pain medicine, he declined. Instead, he got under the covers as he had every night before but this time he was awake and alert. When she finally stepped out from behind the blanket she'd hung as a dressing screen and climbed into bed beside him, he reached out and touched her face. Hannah looked over at him and he smiled. "Hannah Coppersmith, while this bullet and storm may have forced us into a situation where we'll have to marry, I want you to know that I'm glad it's you I'm going to have to marry. No, that's not right. I'm not glad; I'm down right thrilled with the idea of making you Mrs. Wheeler."

Then he leaned over the wall of quilts and kissed her. With every second the kiss lingered, he poured more passion into it. He felt Bob land between them and with his other hand grabbed the rooster and flung him from the bed. Pulling her as close to him as the quilts would allow, he didn't gentle the kiss or pull back till he felt the bird land just above his head ready to attack. Then he pulled back and glared at the rooster. "Soon, Bob, you'll be sleeping outside and she'll be all mine." The rooster looked him in the eye before letting out a loud crow and then settling between them as if to say, "Soon, but not tonight."

Hannah blushed and her fingers went to her lips. Henry knew she had a good idea what he had tried to convey to her with that kiss. Soon he'd say the words but not till he knew she'd believe them.

∼

HANNAH LAY AWAKE LONG after Henry had fallen asleep. She

could still feel his kiss; it felt different than any of the ones he'd given her during the six days they'd been alone. Those others had made her a quivering mass of woman but this kiss had felt like he was claiming her very soul. It was a kiss that said there was more to his feelings than friendship or even desire; it said she was his and he was hers. He'd caught Bob in mid-attack and flung him away. He'd pulled her as close to him as he could before letting her go as if to tell her that something had changed between them. He hadn't said he loved her but that kiss said it for him. He'd told Bob that she was his. He'd told her he wanted to marry her. She really was getting her heart's desire here.

If she could just be convinced beyond a shadow of a doubt that he had nothing left of Esther in his heart, she'd give back as passionately as he'd given. So here she lay as the fire burned down and Henry slept, wondering if she'd ever know for certain that her sister's memory didn't lay between them as surely as the roll of quilts did. She'd almost convinced herself to settle down and go to sleep when she realized that once again someone stood at the foot of her bed. "Penny, what are you doing here?"

"I need your help again, Hannah. I have another charge here in Creede and she is in need of your services tonight. Please dress and grab your medical bag."

Hannah climbed out of the bed and began to dress. "Penny, I know that the trail should be cleared enough to travel tomorrow afternoon, but it will be way too treacherous tonight."

"Don't worry about travel. I've gotten that taken care of for you. Someone will remember later that they sent for you and gave you a ride there and back, but I'll take you to the girl. Just be ready; she's at the Golden Nugget."

"Maybe you should go to Doctor Thomas and take him."

Penny shook her head. "I can't. I'm not allowed to show myself to anyone but you, Hannah dear."

Hannah pulled on her coat and grabbed her medical bag. "Henry will be very upset if he wakes and I'm not here."

"Don't worry about your man. He won't wake till morning; my Boss has seen to that. Now take my hand and, whatever happens, don't let go till we are outside the Golden Nugget. They are waiting for you to show up so they'll take you straight to the girl."

"What do you mean, don't let go?"

Penny smiled as they stepped outside. "I wouldn't want to lose you along the way." Then Hannah gasped as she was flying through the sky as fast as a thought. Before she could get used to the sensation, she was on her feet just down the boardwalk from the newly erected Golden Nugget Saloon. Penny smiled at her. "Here you are, safe and sound. Just come find me here when you're ready to return to the cabin."

"You aren't coming with me?"

"I told you I'm not allowed to let anyone else see me. But Celeste is also my project and I couldn't leave her to suffer when I knew you could help her."

Hannah nodded and walked up and into the saloon like it was an everyday occurrence. She stepped inside and was greeted by one of the soiled doves. "I knew you'd come if we sent for you. It's Celeste; she's been beat real bad, Miss."

Hannah's teeth clenched. "Take me to her."

The girl nodded and led Hannah upstairs to a room on the end. Hannah stepped inside and froze at the sight before her. Standing beside the girl crumpled in a heap on the floor stood the one person she thought she'd never have to put eyes on again as long as she lived: her sister's killer and husband, Augustus Rayner. His eyes got real big. "Who is this, Jose?"

"This is Nurse Hannah. She works for Doctor Thomas, Gus. I told you she'd come help with Celeste."

"I see. Okay, you get on back downstairs and get to work; I'll see to the nurse and Celeste."

The calico queen looked like she wanted to argue but she nodded her head and left without a word.

"Well, well, well. If it isn't little Hannah Coppersmith all grown up."

"I know who you are, too, Augustus. But that doesn't matter right now; helping this girl does. Put her on the bed and then leave me to my work."

Her brother-in-law grabbed her by the arm. "Don't get all high and mighty on me, girl. This is my place. These are my girls and if it hadn't been for that fire and Dougal messing up, you'd be one of my girls right now."

"I'm not getting anything with you. I don't even want to be in the same room with you. But Celeste needs my help so get her on the bed and let me get to work or you might have one less girl to run."

He let her arm go, picked the woman up from the floor, and dumped her on the bed. "Do what you can and then we'll talk."

He walked out. Hannah took a deep breath before starting to examine the girl on the bed. She was young for a soiled dove and had only come to town a few weeks ago. Someone had beat her but not where it would show and cause her not to attract customers. Mostly, she was just bruised and had a few deep lacerations on her back from what looked like a whip. Hannah cleaned them and sewed them up. She found a lump on the back of the woman's head as if someone had slammed her head into the floor.

Hannah got her awake with some smelling salts and checked her eyes to make sure they were okay. Then she asked the girl what had happened. "I was asked by Doctor Thomas to help look after the Reverend after he almost got hung. I missed a couple of paying customers and Gus wasn't happy."

Hannah was mad now. The man had beat this woman same as he'd done her sister; if he'd killed her no one would have said anything. Well, she knew what to do about that. "I'm going to give you a dose of laudanum for your pain and leave you a bottle. No more than three or four drops in a glass of water every four hours, Celeste."

"Okay, thank you for coming to help me, Miss Hannah."

"Why do you work here? I'm sure we could find you a better job."

"Oh no, ma'am, this is all I'm good for. I been used for a while now; no one wants a ruined woman anywhere but where I am."

Hannah looked down at the girl with the olive skin and dark hair and eyes. Even after such horrors there was still an innocence about her. "Don't you believe that, Celeste. I know that God has great plans for you. Why, I bet you have one of the best angels he has on your side."

"No, Miss Hannah, I don't think God even knows who I am."

"That's not true. You just keep praying and watch; God's got a plan for you, Celeste. You'll see."

The door opened and Gus came in. "I see you got her awake. Get dressed, girl, and get downstairs; you got money to make up."

Hannah put herself between Gus and Celeste. "She can't work tonight or tomorrow, either. Whoever beat her did too good a job; she needs to rest for a few days until her stitches come out. She can serve drinks after tomorrow but the head injury means she needs to be in bed for two days. Otherwise, she could get worse."

"She needs to be downstairs earning her keep."

"In two days she can serve; six before she can go back to her other duties. Either you see to it or I'll have Doc come tell Mr. Anders you rejected our medical advice."

Gus's eyes narrowed. "Fine. Two nights and no whoring for a week."

Hannah nodded, "Good. Let's go and let her rest."

She walked past Gus, trying not to shake from anger or fear. She left the room and he followed her. Before she could get downstairs, his hand clamped down on her arm again and pulled her into an empty room. "Now then, let's talk about you and me."

"There's nothing to talk about."

Gus smiled; it wasn't a pleasant smile. "Not true, sister-in-law. What are you doing in Creede?"

"I'm a nurse working with Doctor Thomas. What are you doing in Creede? Shouldn't you still be running from a hangman's noose?

Gus squeezed her arm. "See, this is what we need to talk about. I'm Gus Reed and I work for the Golden Nugget. If I even think you're telling people differently, I'll have to make sure you get to visit your sister real soon."

Hannah laughed. "I don't have to say anything. Obviously, you haven't heard Creede has a U.S. Marshal here investigating Archie and the Sheriff and the kidnapping of those of us taken before the fire. He gets one good look at you and you'll be heading to New York and that noose faster than you can blink."

Gus shook his head. "Doubt it; ain't no paper on me in this town or state. I've checked."

Hannah grinned. "Won't have to be. This Marshal knows you, Augustus. Knows you real well. His name is Henry Wheeler."

Gus laughed. "Wheeler? No one's seen him in a week. Rumor was he got shot and is buried under a snowdrift somewhere. Even if he ain't, Wheeler is a weak, sniveling fop. He wouldn't fight for your sister before we were married and he won't fight now. You just worry about yourself, little sister, else I'll introduce you to the things I did to your sister before I end you the same way I did her. As a matter of fact, I might just make you my second wife. I always did want to sample your goods as well but your sister kept you away from me." He reached out to pull her toward the bed when the door opened and in tumbled Jose and a miner. "Oh sorry. Didn't realize the room was occupied."

Hannah pulled away and exited quickly. "It's all yours, Jose, Gus was just getting the rundown on Celeste."

She quickly walked down the stairs and was headed for the door when Mr. Anders stopped her. "Nurse Coppersmith. You tended to Celeste?"

She smiled. This man made her skin crawl, too, but at least he had never done anything to make her think he was anything other than a rich man making money. "Yes, sir. She needs to stay in bed for two days and no whoring till the stitches in her back come out. Send her to see me or Doctor Thomas in six days and one of us will remove them."

The man nodded and handed her a double eagle coin. "Much obliged. I'll see to it. Your ride is waiting?"

"It is, Mr. Anders. I should go; it's too cold to make them wait."

The man nodded and she hurried out and down the boardwalk. When Penny appeared and took her hand, Hannah let out a sigh of relief. "Did you know?"

"Of course I did. What are you going to do?"

"Nothing for now. Henry will insist on coming with me for my first appointment to check the girls. He'll see him and that will be that."

"That choice is yours but remember that you made the choice. Just remember, if you need me, call for me."

Then they were flying again and before Hannah could even catch her breath she was back inside her cabin and Penny was gone. Hannah slipped into her nightgown, pulled the extra covers off the bed, and removed the rolled quilts, too. She climbed under all the covers and snuggled up as close as she could against Henry. Bob looked at her from the bottom bed post. "I know Bob, but I need him to hold me." She pulled Henry's arm over her and he unconsciously pulled her close, holding her tight just like she needed. She lay there and shook till his scent and warmth calmed her and she slipped into a troubled sleep.

9

Henry woke the next morning to find his body wrapped around Hannah's. She was under the covers with him, pressed right up against his body and his arms and legs were wrapped over her. He started to unwind himself and pull away but she whispered and scooted closer to him. "Hannah, honey, what are you doing?"

"Just hold me a little longer, Henry. Please. I had bad dreams and needed you to hold me. You did and I just want to keep feeling safe in your arms."

Henry kissed the back of her head. "If you're sure, honey. I didn't want to upset you. Do you want to tell me what your dreams were?"

"I dreamed someone was trying to hurt me like Esther got hurt. I just needed to feel your arms around me and know you had me."

He pulled her tighter to him even though he knew it wasn't appropriate. "I will always have you. No one will hurt you as long as I'm breathing, Hannah."

"I know; that's why I wanted you to hold me."

"I'll hold you anytime you want me to or anytime you'll let me. I'm more surprised that your rooster isn't pitching a fit."

"I told you, Henry, Bob is special; he knows his job is to protect my virtue and he knew it was safe and still is. If he thought you were trying to take advantage of me I have no doubt you'd be feeling his wrath."

"Then I'm glad he understands. Should we just lay here for a bit or are you ready to get up?"

She shuddered and held on to his arm. "Could we just lay here a little longer?"

"Hannah, we can lay here as long as you want. But I got to say I'm finding a way to get us to town today. We need to see the preacher right quick after this."

She giggled and then sighed. "Are you sure, Henry? I mean, you don't have to marry me. I'm tough; I would survive anything anyone said."

He pulled her so that she would turn and face him and wrapped his arm back around her. "Are you telling me you don't want to marry me, Hannah?"

"I didn't say that."

He looked into her gray eyes and tilted her head so she could see his eyes better. "Listen carefully, Hannah Coppersmith. There is nothing I want more than to make you my wife. Not because I have to, but because I need to. I can't see my life without you right here where you are now. In my bed, in my arms and in my life every day and every night. So let me just ask you. Will you go to town with me today and marry me?"

"That's what I want, too, Henry. Yes, I'll go to town and marry you today."

Henry pulled her tightly against him and captured her mouth for a kiss that was even more intense than the one they'd shared the night before. He knew he should be ashamed of the way he was pressed against Hannah from foot to head and everywhere in between, but he wasn't. If he was honest, it felt perfect and right and like they belonged together just like they were. They both might have forgotten themselves in the moment if not for the flutter of wings and the loud crow that came from the foot of the bed. Henry pulled away and smiled at Hannah. "That, I believe, is my warning that Bob has decided it's time for us to get up before he goes after my body parts with that beak of death of his."

Hannah giggled again and gave Henry another quick kiss before rolling away from him to get dressed. "I need to look at your stitches today before you get your shirt on, Henry. I think they should be ready to come out. I'm sure you're ready to have use of your hands and guns back."

Henry nodded and turned away from her so she could have modesty to walk behind the blanket to get dressed.

HANNAH COULDN'T BELIEVE it when Henry had asked her to marry him. He didn't have to do that because they'd already agreed to get married. But the fact that he'd asked her in such a romantic way while holding her and assuring her he'd always keep her safe. It was beyond her wildest dreams. He still hadn't said he loved her but he'd made sure she knew how he felt.

After dressing she'd gotten her scissors and quickly removed his stitches. The wound was well on its way to being healed. She cautioned him to take it easy getting back to his normal routine just to give it more time to heal completely. Even as she said it she knew he would push just as far as he could.

Dressed, they enjoyed breakfast and then while she put the cabin to some semblance of order, Henry went out to hitch her mare to her wagon. They'd agreed to come back there tonight and then move to Topaz the next day. Henry had wrapped himself in one of Hannah's bear skins since his coat hadn't been salvageable after she'd cut it off him. No sooner had he come into the cabin to let her know they were ready to ride into town than they heard the sound of someone coming up the trail and a, "Hello, the cabin."

Henry's Colts were already back around his waist and he picked up the rifle as he and Hannah walked to the door. There, in a buggy much like Hannah's, was Doctor Thomas, Reverend Theodore, and Reverend and Millie Bing. "Hello, come on in. We were just coming to see some of you."

Doctor Thomas was the first to speak. "Marshal, it's good to see you; we were worried about you. Sheriff Ketchem said you'd taken a bullet saving Reverend Theodore, but when you never made it to my cabin we thought the worst."

"Sorry to worry you but I knew I wasn't going to be able to make it to your place. Thought I might make it here to Hannah's but that didn't happen either. Passed out at the turn to the trail to her place."

"How did you end up here, then?"

Hannah took up the story. "I was heading out to celebrate the new year when I came across him and his horse in the middle of the trail. I got him back here and removed the bullet." She made no mention of the help she'd had or anything else but it was obvious everyone realized what that meant. Only Reverend Theodore was angry enough to speak of it. "Are you saying, woman, that you've had this man in your home and bed since New Year's Eve?"

"He has. I took a slug out of his back and sewed him up. He'd lost a lot of blood and, with the blizzard, I knew I couldn't move him again without killing him."

Theodore climbed down from the buggy and placed himself right in front of her, inches from her face. "That would have been better than living in sin with the man for a week."

Henry's eyes tightened. "Excuse me? Are you accusing Miss Coppersmith of something, Reverend?"

"I'm not accusing; I'm saying she has ruined her reputation and sinned against God by taking you into her house without a chaperone."

"We had a chaperone," Henry said. Theodore looked at him, finally surprised.

"You did? Whom?"

"Bob was our chaperone and a great job he did of it, too."

The young pastor's face turned purple with anger. "Are you telling me this harlot was alone with two men for a week?"

Henry opened his mouth to call the man to task for his slur to Hannah's good name but before he could, there was a series of loud clucks. The good reverend shrieked like a little girl as Bob tore into his head with wings and beak and spurs. "Get it off me!" He screamed and waved his arms but Bob had gotten his talons in the Reverends hair and was beating him about the ears with his wings and pecking at the top of his head with his beak. Everyone else came down from the buggy and were attempting to get the reverend away from the rooster. After the man had dropped to his knees, Henry finally called out. "That's enough, Bob, I think he knows not to slander Miss Hannah again."

The rooster immediately hopped off the man's head and actually defecated on the reverend's shoes, walked a few steps away, turned and looked up at the preacher as he puffed out as much as he could and let forth a hearty COCK-A-DOODLE-DO!! The Reverend jumped back and covered his head with his hands as if afraid the rooster was about to attack again. Henry looked the Reverend in the eye. "As you can see, Bob is very protective of Hannah. I assure you that nothing untoward happened under his watchful eyes or beak.

"However, I am going to say this, Reverend. Your near hanging didn't teach you anything, did it? You better learn to curb that tongue of yours or the next time I see a mob trying to hang you, I might just ride on by."

MILLIE HAD TAKEN Hannah in her arms and the two were off to the side talking. Henry looked at the Doctor and the other minister. "Either of you want to chance angering Hannah's protector?"

The doctor shook his head. "She said you were shot?"

"Yeah, in the back. She patched me up."

"Would you mind if I took a look to make sure?"

"No, come on in the cabin and I'll let ya see."

The doctor nodded; he and Reverend Bing started toward the cabin. Reverend Theodore startled when Bob flew up and flapped his wings in the man's face and he froze. "I don't believe the bird will allow me to pass. "

Henry laughed and nodded. "I reckon you're right,

Reverend. Maybe you'd better just stand real still so Bob doesn't think you're trying to attack Miss Coppersmith again."

Still chuckling, Henry entered the cabin and undid his buttons. The doctor checked and probed the wound. "Looks very good; she did an excellent job."

Henry agreed and told the doctor so. Then Callum Bing cleared his throat. "Henry, you know what is going to be expected of you after spending the week alone in Miss Coppersmith's home?"

Henry nodded. "We both do, Callum. We were actually on our way to see you when you pulled up. I asked her to marry me this morning and she agreed."

"Well then, good. Don't get me wrong, lad. I'm glad the lassie patched you up, but I'm even more pleased you agreed to do the right thing. The woman's been through enough at the hands of the men of Creede without having to go through what would have happened if you'd refused."

"I promised to keep her safe, Reverend, and I plan to spend my life keeping it."

"Well, if the doctor and my sister will stand as witnesses we can marry you both right here."

"Then let's go see what the women have to add. I need to go see Ketchem, too."

"Why's that?"

"Because, Doctor, I've looked at it every way I can and the only person I can come up with that shot me in the back is Ketchem."

"Are you sure? I mean, I know he bends the law for Anders from time to time but attacking a U.S. Marshal; that's a death sentence."

"I am fairly certain. Letting him see me alive and making

sure he knows I'm going to be looking for the man who shot me might be enough to get him to mess up."

"Well, let's go get you wed so the two of you can do what you need to do today."

With that the three men exited the cabin to get the women and have a wedding.

10

Hannah watched as Henry went inside the cabin with Doctor Thomas and Reverend Bing. Bob was still riled up and wouldn't allow Reverend Theodore to move at all. She turned her attention back to Millie who had been talking to her. "I'm sorry, Millie, what were you saying?"

The other woman smiled and patted her arm. "It doesn't matter now. You've answered my question without saying a word. I wanted to be sure you were okay with what was going to inevitably happen here, but I can see that you're completely in love with Marshal Wheeler and my concerns are unfounded."

Hannah blushed. "I am in love with him. I've been in love with the idea of him since I was seventeen."

Millie looked at her in surprise. "Oh? I didn't realize you and the Marshal knew each other that long."

Hannah nodded, "We grew up just a few blocks from each other. He courted my sister for a while."

Millie's eyebrows rose in surprise. "Yet you claim you've been in love with the idea of him since you were seventeen?"

Hannah sighed; she hadn't wanted to have to tell this story again. "Yes, while he was seeing my sister we had several occasions to talk. He was going to take over his father's store back then. I always wanted to become a nurse and told anyone who'd listen that I was going to go to nursing school when I finished school. My mother was determined that my sister and I would marry well, but I didn't want that. Henry was the only person back then that listened to my dreams and took them seriously. He encouraged me to follow them. I was heartbroken when my sister accepted another suitor's proposal and Henry stopped coming to our house. Then we'd heard he'd gone west as a Deputy Marshal. I never thought to see him again."

"And you are okay with the fact that you're about to marry one of your sister's suitors?"

Hannah blushed and then nodded. "My sister was never serious about Henry. She even laughed in his face when he proposed to her. He wasn't from a wealthy enough family for my sister. My only concern was that he still was in love with my sister. He's shown me that he is not."

Millie's eyes got wide. "What are ya tellin' me, Hannah? Was Reverend Theodore right in his assumptions?"

Hannah glared at her friend and the sister of the pastor everyone liked. "No! Nothing happened like you are thinking. You know me better than that, Millie. Henry is barely healed from his wound and loss of blood. Besides, I planned to come to my marriage bed pure and Bob has been very protective of Henry getting too close. But we've had time to talk and share our thoughts and fears and dreams this past week. That was all I meant."

Millie nodded and hugged Hannah. "Good, I didna think you'd allow the man liberties, but I've heard that love makes people act as they shouldn't sometimes. My other concern is what will your sister think of all this?"

"Esther is dead. The man she chose over Henry killed her about a year after their wedding."

"I'm sorry; I didn't know."

Hannah shook her head. "Nothing to be sorry about. No reason for you to know; it's not like I talk about it. I worry a bit about what Mother will think, but at this point she'll probably be happy that I got married."

Just then the men came out and headed their direction. Reverend Theodore fell in step with them. Bob was right on his heels making his presence known. When they all got to where she and Millie were standing, Reverend Bing turned to her. "Henry has told me the two of you talked and were coming into town to get married today. Is that true?"

Hannah moved over to Henry who put his arm around her shoulders. "Yes, Reverend."

"Then if there are no objections, I'll conduct the ceremony now and we can go into town and sign the license when we are finished."

"Absolutely not!" Reverend Theodore bellowed. "Reverend Bing, I insist that they be placed in church discipline and be forced to live separate for a time before they are married. That is the proper and Christian thing to do. Otherwise we are just giving God's approval to living in sin."

Henry let go of Hannah and stepped up to the younger minister. "I believe you, sir, need a lesson in tact. Perhaps I should join Bob in teaching you that lesson."

The younger man gasped. "You would threaten to lay hands on a man of God?"

Henry laughed in the other man's face. "A man of God? Is that what you think you are? Let me tell you something, Eugene. I spent the last four years working alongside

Reverend Nathan Ryder and spent plenty of time in the company of Reverend David Ryder, both of whom like Reverend Bing here, I consider to be men of God. You, sir, are nothing more than a Pharisee and a man using the office of minister to make himself more important."

"How dare you, sir!"

"NO! How dare you, sir. A true man of God is one who remembers that without love, even speaking God's word is but a sounding gong and a crashing cymbal." Henry turned and looked at Reverend Bing. "I hate to delay being married but I will not allow this man to be present to ruin what is supposed to be a happy time for Hannah and me. So with your permission I'll take Hannah into town and get the supplies we need and if you, Doctor Thomas, and your sister will meet us at your church in Bachelor this evening, we'll marry there without him!" Henry pointed at Eugene.

Callum Bing looked at Doctor Thomas and Millie, both of whom nodded. "That's fine, Marshal. Only I would urge you to marry today; it would be the best thing for Hannah and your reputations."

Hannah smiled as Henry looked at her. "Reverend, I don't give a hoot about my reputation but I'm not waiting one more day to make this beautiful and kind woman my wife. We'll see you this afternoon." Theodore opened his mouth, Hannah was sure to protest once more, but just then Bob started clucking and pecking at the man's legs as high as he could reach without leaving the ground. Eugene screeched and started running for the buggy they'd all come in with Bob running after him clucking and flapping his wings right on his heels. "I believe Bob is telling Reverend Theodore it's time for us to be going," Millie said, trying hard not to laugh. As Doctor Thomas looked at Hannah, she could see disappointment for a brief moment on his face.

"Yes, it seems like he is. Shall we drop the Reverend off at his church and go prepare for Miss Coppersmith's wedding?"

The others nodded and the three of them moved to the buggy at a slower pace. Once they were all settled, Doctor Thomas nodded to her and Henry, and then turned the buggy and headed back the way they came.

"Let's head into town as well. I want to go by the mercantile and grab a new coat and some supplies we'll need in Topaz. Get what you want at the store, Hannah, there isn't much food wise at my place. Even if we aren't going to head that way till tomorrow, it would be wise to plan ahead."

She smiled and nodded. He stopped and put his hands on her waist as if to help her into the buggy, but instead pulled her against him. She tilted her head back as his drew near to her and once again she was lost in his kiss, right up till Bob crowed a loud Cock-a-doodle-do, then Henry released her lips and helped her into the buggy. She heard him talking to Bob as he came around to the other side. "Your task is almost done, Bob. I won't put up with you interrupting me after we say our vows."

Henry climbed up beside her and reached for the reins. They both were startled when Bob hopped up onto the rear seat with a loud cluck and then settled in the middle. "I guess he means to see us to the church."

Hannah gigged, "Well, it wouldn't be right to get married and not have our chaperone present after all he's done for us."

Henry's eyes showed his humor at the situation. "No, and if Bob's there we can be sure Reverend Theodore won't be."

"No, not if he's smart he won't."

With that Hannah snuggled close to Henry and with a snap of the reins they were headed into Creede.

Henry basked in the feel of Hannah holding on to his arm and snuggling in close on the ride to Creede. For him the trip was over too soon. He shrugged out of the bear fur in front of the mercantile and then helped Hannah down. He looked at Bob. "You stay here and watch over the buggy, Bob. We'll be back as soon as we are done getting supplies."

The ornery rooster clucked and ruffled his feathers as if to say okay. Henry was amazed again at Hannah's curious bird. If he didn't know better he'd think that it understood every word spoken to it. He turned and walked arm in arm with Hannah into the mercantile. Mortimer's new bride, Toria, was behind the counter which meant that Mortimer was probably upstairs having his lunch and Tom was either with him or on a delivery. Mrs. Jackson looked up when they came in. "Hello, Marshal, it's good to see that the rumor of your death was wrong."

Henry smiled. "Yes, I'm sorry to say I'm still alive and kicking. Just took a while to heal enough to get around."

"So you were shot then? We had wondered when you never turned up anywhere."

"I was lucky that Nurse Coppersmith found me and was able to fix me up. However, it was at the cost of that lovely coat you'd sold me. Would you happen to have another one?"

Toria nodded. "We do, I believe it's hanging back there beside the scarves and gloves that Mrs. Clark has been making for us."

"I'm much obliged. Hannah will be getting some supplies. I'm going to go over and let Ketchem know I'm alive; I'll return and settle up with you if that's all right."

"That's fine, Marshal. If we can't trust the law to pay their bill, who can we trust?"

Henry chuckled, knowing that Toria was picking on him. He could also see the curiosity behind her eyes and knew that as soon as he left she'd be asking Hannah for the reason he was buying her supplies. Henry found the coat; it fit just like the last one so he left it on as he walked over to Hannah. "If there is a dress back there in the women's section that you'd like for a wedding dress, get it."

Hannah smiled at him. "I'm fine as I am."

"I know that, but this is the only time you're going to marry if I have any say about it, so just look and if you find one you like, get it please."

"Since you put it that way, I'll look."

Toria Jackson was lit up with the news she'd overheard and said, "Oh, Hannah, Vivian just sent in a new gown I think would make the perfect wedding dress for you. I haven't even gotten it out yet. Come see." The two women headed for the back room and Henry used that opportunity to slip out the door and head over to the sheriff's office.

When he reached the jail, he slipped the hammer thong off his Peacemakers just in case. He was convinced that the only person who could have shot him was Ketchem and the fact that the man had been telling people he had been shot and was most likely dead seemed to be the final verification Henry needed. He couldn't arrest the man without proof but he planned to let him know he was still alive and more determined than ever to prove the sheriff was crooked and would add attempted murder of a U.S. Marshal to the crimes he was investigating. Once he was ready, Henry opened the door of the jail and stepped inside, sliding to the right and keeping the wall behind his back.

Black Jack when he heard Henry entering the office,

turned white as a sheet. "Marshal, we thought you were dead when you didn't turn up for a week."

"Sorry to disappoint ya, Jack."

"Not disappointed, relieved actually. Didn't want to have to wire Marshal Ryder and have the Preacher back in my town again." He indicated the chair in front of his desk. "Have a seat. Want some coffee."

Henry smiled. "I'm fine standing, thank you, and I don't need any coffee. Just wanted to check in and let you know I'm still alive. Nurse Coppersmith removed the bullet and sewed me up. I've been snowed in and recovering since. Doc just checked the wound himself this morning; said she did a right nice job of it."

"Well, that's good. We all figured you'd died trying to get help. Glad you didn't."

"I'm sure you are. I'll be back at my investigation next week but wanted to ask you if you got any leads on who shot me in the back or if you'd arrested Archie for trying to lynch the Reverend. I can see you didn't."

Jack shook his head. "The snow made finding any tracks of who might have shot at us impossible.. Lucky for you I came along when I did or they might have finished the job."

"Umm hmm. And Archie?"

Ketchem held his hands out in the innocent pose. "I know you think that he was one of the instigators but Mr. Anders and a ton of other witnesses all say he was at the Golden Nugget all night that night. I think you were mistaken."

"Then I guess that tells me what I need to know about your choice, doesn't it? If I were you I'd be thinking of making a change Ketchem, won't take me long to get the evidence I need to prove you're in Ander's pocket. Since you don't seem too concerned with investigating my shooting,

I'll just have to look into that myself, too. By the way, do you still have that derringer you used to brag about keeping in your vest pocket?"

Ketchem's face turned even more pale. "Um... no, I lost that two weeks ago in a card game over at the Nugget."

"I see. Who'd you lose it to? I'd like to talk to him since I was shot with a small caliber weapon like a derringer."

"New guy named Gus Reed, runs Anders' upstairs for him."

"Better hope he backs your story, Jack. Attempted murder of a Marshal is a hanging offense."

"Now see here. I fired on whoever it was that shot at us. Remember I was there in the line of fire, too."

Henry leaned off the wall and let his hands fall to rest on his gun belt just behind each holster. "Were you? As I recall, you were behind me when that shot rang out. Funny how I got shot in the back and you didn't even get a scratch."

"What are you insinuating?"

"I think you know what I'm saying, Black Jack, You better hope that Reed fella backs your claim and can show me that derringer. Else I'll be back and slap cuffs on you."

"Now see here, there's no call for that."

"Just giving you fair warning, Ketchem. One way or another you'll end up behind my bars soon and Creede will be better off for it. Now if you will excuse me, I need to go to the saloon and then fetch my bride to go see Reverend Bing."

"Your bride? Who you marrying?"

"None of your business now, is it, sheriff? I'll be seeing ya soon. Lucky for you I got an appointment with the Reverend or I'd be hauling you away today, I bet."

Ketchem stood and reached down, only to be looking at the barrel of Henry's right hand Colt. "Now you wouldn't have been thinking of trying to shoot me again, would you, Jack?"

"I have never shot you, Marshal, and I think it's time for you to leave my office unless you have proof."

"Oh, I'll leave and return with proof. I'm just curious if you'll try to shoot me again before then. Would save the judge a lot of trouble if you did try again."

Henry slid over to the door, opened it, and backed out. Then he spun to put his back to the wall outside the jail while he pulled the door closed behind him. He looked up and down the street making sure there were plenty of people in sight and then turned and keeping one eye alert for movement behind him, made his way over to the Golden Nugget. He'd see if he could meet this Gus Reed and check out the sheriff's story before Ketchem had a chance to arrange an alibi with another of Anders' employees.

11

Hannah followed Toria into the back room. She knew the first question the sweet shopkeeper was going to ask her, and smiled when she did. "Okay spill, how did you land the Marshal for a husband? I didn't even know the two of you knew each other."

"Henry and I go way back. I knew him when we lived in New York City. His parents ran the shop my mother loved to shop in the most. So you could say I've known him most of my life."

The shopkeeper's brown eyes flashed with irritation. "That's not what I'm asking and you know it. How did you and he end up on the way to the altar?"

While she was speaking, she'd been looking through the items stored in the back room.

Hannah didn't know why but she told Toria the whole story about being awakened New Year's Eve by a woman at the foot of her bed, going with the woman to rescue Henry, seeing the angel of death, and learning the woman was her guardian angel and the deceased grandmother of a friend of hers. She told her about Bob, the attack rooster, and everything that had happened the past seven days.

When she was finished she almost passed out when Toria hugged her and said. "Welcome to the club. Several of us ladies have gotten together and realized that there seems to be some spiritual power helping us find our true loves. For me it was Mortimer's first wife. She thought I'd be perfect for her husband and son, and be the help and healing they needed. She also thought they'd be perfect for me. I must say I agree with her. So I'll pray your angel is as successful as mine has been. Oh, and I want to meet this attack chicken; he sounds like a real character."

Hannah smiled. "He is. You should have seen him today when Reverend Theodore got all judgmental and preachy. He went after him and afterwards wouldn't let him move a muscle. When he tried to insist Henry and I not be married today, Bob ran him right back to his buggy."

Both women were laughing at that. Toria held up a beautiful deep crimson gown made from strips of material, creating a layered-look gown that was beautiful. It matched the exact shade of Hannah's wool coat, too. "Oh, this is perfect."

"I thought it would be. Hurry, go behind the screen there and try it on. Let's see if it's going to fit you like I think it will."

Hannah took the dress, put it on, and came out to show Mrs. Jackson. "Hannah, it's like it was made for you."

Hannah nodded. "I shouldn't get it, but Henry was pretty adamant about me buying a dress for the wedding, wasn't he?"

Tori smiled. "He was, and honestly Hannah, I think Viv made it for you. She didn't know she was making it for you, but it's the perfect size and coloring for you. Maybe your angel inspired her to make it so you'd have the perfect gown for your speedy wedding."

Hannah slipped behind the screen again and changed back into her day dress and nurses apron. She handed it to Toria. "I'll take it. Would you wrap it so Henry doesn't see it till I put it on for the wedding?"

The shopkeeper nodded. "Listen, before we go back and get your supplies I wanted to ask you if you have any questions about your wedding night? I know a lot of women have never been told what to expect."

Hannah blushed. "I'm a nurse and a midwife, Toria. I know what to expect, and I've worked with the saloon girls enough to know it isn't all unpleasant either."

Her last statement caused the shopkeeper to blush as well. "That's um... good then. Let's go get the other supplies you need and I'll wrap this dress for you."

They went back and Hannah began gathering the things she would need once she moved to Henry's. She didn't know what pans or dishes he'd have so she got a Dutch oven, a skillet, a stew pot, a set of plates, and cutlery. She got a cutting board, a serving platter, fork and carving knife, as well as a paring knife. She also got a set of six enamel mugs so they'd have two upstairs; Henry could take the rest down to the jail if he needed them. Then she stocked up on things like flour, salt, sugar, cornmeal, coffee, beans, several tins of peaches, some dried apples, and any other staples she thought they'd need. She knew she'd need to see what Henry had and how they were laid out in Topaz before she ordered anything else. "I don't know what else to get so I'll stop there for now and come back my first day working at the clinic."

"What do you mean your first day? I thought you and Doctor Thomas were already working together. I know several people were already speculating on when the two of you would be getting married. Won't they all be surprised."

Hannah smiled. "Well, Henry and I had a talk about where we would live and work. After all, his office is set up in Topaz and he has an apartment there above the jail. I was renting a line shack from the Morgan's and working for Doctor Thomas. Henry and I agreed he had the better place to live, but he was worried about my traveling such a distance alone twice a day, every day. I agreed to arrange with Doctor Thomas to come into the office once a week to do the ladies' appointments he needs me to do. I'll be able to visit my pregnant women at their homes, and we will talk to Mr. Jameson about telegraphs in case of emergencies like babies coming, or if one of the women at the saloons needs my help."

"Well, I hope you won't be a stranger living over in Topaz. We'd miss you around here."

Hannah nodded. "No, there aren't as many shops in Topaz so I'm sure we'll be here a lot. And like I said, I'll be at the clinic one day a week so I'll shop on those days."

Just then the door opened and Henry came in. When he saw the amount of stuff she'd bought, he smiled. "We might not be able to haul all this in your buggy, Hannah."

She frowned. "Oh, I hadn't thought about that. We might need to rent a wagon from the livery."

Toria looked at them. "Are you planning to ride to Topaz tonight after the wedding?"

Henry shook his head. "No, going to spend tonight at Hannah's cabin. I thought we'd wait till tomorrow to head for Topaz."

"Well, if you don't mind paying, I could have Tom and Willie deliver this stuff there tomorrow afternoon."

Henry looked at Hannah who nodded. "There are a few

things I got to replenish the line shack, but the rest could go to Topaz."

"Well then, get what goes to the cabin and I'll load it, and then we'll head up to Bachelor and get married."

Hannah quickly pointed to the things she wanted at the cabin, and Henry wasted no time in loading them in the buggy. Hannah took the package with her dress and a surprise she'd bought for her wedding night tonight, and Toria congratulated them just as Mortimer was coming into the store. When he heard of their wedding he offered his congratulations, too. "Here I'd been thinking about carrying Miss Elizabeth's matrimonial times paper, but seems like the good men of Creede are doing well enough without a mail order bride. Well except me, and I'm very pleased with my mail order bride." He hugged Toria who blushed and laughed. "Behave Mortimer, or I won't make you those cookies you love for dessert tonight."

"Now there's no reason to be cruel, Toria my dear."

Hannah and Henry left laughing at the two of them. Henry helped her up onto the buggy and quickly climbed in and turned them toward Bachelor. As they passed the jail his hand rested on his left hand pistol causing Hannah to wonder about his meeting with the sheriff. But soon enough they were headed up the trail to Reverend Bing's church, and all she could think about was that she was about to become Mrs. Henry Wheeler."

HENRY HELPED Hannah out of the buggy with Bob following behind them. He didn't know how Reverend Bing would feel about having a rooster in the house of God, but if he looked upset, Henry would just toss Bob outside. As they got close to the church and the parsonage behind it, Millie stuck her head out the parsonage door and motioned for them to come that way. So Henry and Hannah changed directions and soon arrived at the parsonage where Millie opened the door. "I didn't want to overstep my place here, but I thought you might wish a bath before you say your vows."

Hannah blushed. "That sounds heavenly, Millie. I haven't been able to clean up much with my patient in my home."

Millie nodded, "I thought so. I've got water heated in the kitchen and had Callum pull in the tub earlier. So let's get you all cleaned up and ready for your wedding."

She and Hannah went through to the kitchen and shut the door, leaving Henry standing in the entranceway. Callum and Doctor Thomas approached him and shook his hand. The doctor once again had a look of disappointment or something on his face. "Have I done something to you, Doctor, that has you upset with me?"

The Doc's face registered a moment of shock. "What?? Oh, no, of course not, Marshal Wheeler. It was nothing. I just had kind of built it up in my head that maybe Miss Coppersmith and I would marry. You know, having the medical profession in common and her working alongside me."

Henry felt an unaccustomed moment of jealousy. "Are you telling me that you and Hannah were courting, Doc? Because if so, I'll step back. Nothing happened between us, and I wouldn't want to overstep an agreement you two had."

The Doctor waved his hand. "No, Marshal, there was nothing like that. No formal or even implied commitment between us. It was just something that I'd been thinking on for a few weeks. There is no reason for you to step aside. Especially when it is obvious the two of you are in love."

Henry stilled; his feelings were obvious? He didn't see how; he'd not done anything in front of the men to indicate that anything more than the nurse taking care of her patient had even remotely happened. "I don't know that I'd say that. We get along well enough, and I didn't want her to face ridicule, or more of what Eugene put her through today."

Thomas smiled. "You don't even realize it, do you? You can't be near her without touching her, Wheeler, and when she's out of your reach your eyes never leave her."

Callum laughed and agreed with the doctor. "Aye, lad, you've got it bad; that's for certain. Almost as bad as Hugh had it for our Julianne. He couldn't see it, but the rest of us could. Well, except for Eugene, and honestly I think he saw it too, just couldn't accept the blow to his pride that she didn't want him."

Henry thought about that but didn't say anything about how he felt for Hannah. "You know, I should have bought some new clothes when we were in the mercantile. Here Hannah's going to be all fresh and dressed for our wedding, and I'm in my blood-stained torn shirt and britches."

James Thomas cleared his throat. "I um... hope you aren't offended, but I did notice the condition of your clothes when I examined your wound this morning. I also noticed we looked to be around the same size. If it wouldn't offend you, I did bring a set of my dress clothes with me. I thought you might wish for something better for your wedding."

Henry smiled and clasped the man on the shoulder. "Thank you, Doc, that's right nice of you. I believe I'll take you up on your kind offer." The doctor nodded and went to get the clothes out of his buggy. Henry looked at Reverend Bing. "Do you think Fontaine has the bathhouse open in back of his saloon? I know he's trying to close the saloon, but a good bath wouldn't hurt me neither."

"I believe he has it open still. The saloon, too, though he is trying to sell that. I heard Anders may make him an offer."

"Well, if the bath is open, I'll collect them duds from Doctor Thomas and surprise my wife with a clean and dressed groom."

Henry turned and fairly ran out of the house. He grabbed the clothes that the doctor was bringing him and headed down the road to the saloon. Sure enough, when he told Hugh what was happening the man gave him a towel and bar of soap. "Help yourself, Henry. If you set your boots outside the door, I'll give them a quick clean and polish while you get yourself cleaned up. There's a razor and scissors in the cabinet behind the mirror if you want to shave or trim up."

Henry sat a silver dollar on the bar, took the towel and soap Hugh handed him, and quickly went into the first bathing room in back. He sat his boots outside, hurriedly filled the tub with hot water and cooled it to just a touch over warm and climbed in, washing off the blood, mud and stink of the past week. He climbed out and looked in the mirror and realized his facial hair had grown while he'd been recovering. He opened the cabinet, filled the washbasin, and used the scissors to trim his beard and mustache back to the two-day scruff he preferred. Not clean shaven making him look like a greenhorn, but not the face of a miner or mountain man either.

Once he was done, he slipped into his borrowed clothes and was surprised at how well they fit. While not a suit, it was a pair of dress pants and a white go-to-meeting shirt. The doctor had even included a narrow string bowtie. Henry quickly got the tie tied and opened the door to see his boots clean and shined. He hurried out and thanked Hugh before hurrying down to the church. The Doc was standing outside at the steps up to the church. "Everyone is ready if you are."

"Thanks again, Doc, I appreciate the loan."

"You're welcome; just have Hannah bring them when she comes in to the office next. She talked with me about your arrangement and I agree with you; that ride is too dangerous for her to make alone several times a week. We agreed she'd come to the office on Wednesdays to meet with women who need female medicine. If you can't bring her or if you can't be with her to go to the saloon for the women there, just send me a telegram and I'll come ride with her. We'll keep her safe and doing the work she loves."

Henry shook the man's hand. "Thank you, Doc. I appreciate that."

"You head up to the front and I'll go inform your bride you are ready. Callum is up front already."

Henry walked to the front and waited. He kept looking toward the doors at the back of the church waiting for his first glimpse of Hannah in the dress she'd bought for their wedding. When the door opened and she walked in on the arm of Doctor Thomas, Henry couldn't believe the vision of beauty and desire that came toward him. Her gown was a deep crimson that highlighted the sunset colors of her hair, which was done in those two simple braids she wore so often. He almost lost it when he realized that instead of a bouquet of flowers or some pine boughs, Hannah was carrying Bob. The silly protector was laying in her arm, limp like he was dead, but Henry knew the chicken was alive and Hannah had used him as a bouquet just so she could smuggle him into their wedding. Well, why not? Bob had chaperoned their courtship, as unusual as it was, and he deserved to be in the wedding and see his charge married and his job get handed over to Henry. Then they were beside him and the rooster looked at him with one eye and clucked softly once as if to say he was giving her to Henry.

Reverend Callum saw the rooster and raised an eyebrow, but didn't say anything else. Then he started to speak and Henry tore his attention from Hannah and her rooster companion to the vow he was about to pledge, intent on living up to every single word of them.

12

Hannah was lost in the feelings of her heart as the wedding took place. She was sure she must have said all the right things because the ceremony had gone on, and then before she even could sort out how full her heart was, Reverend Bing looked at Henry and said. "You can kiss your bride, Marshal."

Henry had carefully leaned down with one hand on her cheek and the other laying over top of Bob in her arms. Then he'd kissed her sweetly. Even though it was less passionate than the one they'd shared that morning in bed, it hit her harder. This was her first kiss as Mrs. Henry Wheeler. The first kiss of her dream come true. Then Henry let her go and stepped back. When he stepped back, Bob rose up and hopped out of her arms. He turned and looked back at Henry and Hannah, and then puffed up his chest and crowed out a loud, and Hannah thought, joyous, COCK-A-DOODLE-DOO! Hannah felt like he was giving them his approval; as if to prove she was right, he turned and strutted down the aisle and right out the door.

Millie laughed. "Well, I must say that was certainly the most unusual ending to a wedding."

"I'm just thankful he decided not to peck me for kissing Hannah. That's what he usually does."

Reverend Bing chuckled. "Aye, lad, but you said he was Hannah's protector and chaperone. What did ya think he'd be a doin'? He was keeping the lass safe from the likes of you."

Henry nodded. "Callum, I know Bob is just a rooster, but sometimes I feel as if he's more than just some old ornery bird. Sometimes it almost seems he understands what's being said and done."

The minister slapped Henry on the shoulder. "Well, I would agree with you, lad. I donna think Bob is an ordinary rooster. I don't rightly ken what he is, but he's something special, that's certain-sure."

Hannah fought not to tell them all about Bob and the angel who had brought her and Henry together. She wasn't sure they'd believe her, and she didn't want them all to think she wasn't right in the head. She didn't know why but she knew that Penny wasn't gone yet, and there was something more she had come to do. Something having to do with her and Henry. Because the woman had told her if she needed her to just call out to her. That must mean there would be a reason to call out to her.

Hannah was so caught up in her thoughts that she squealed in surprise when Henry scooped her up into his arms. "Henry Wheeler, you put me down right this minute. You are supposed to ease back into strenuous activities."

Henry laughed. "Strenuous? You think carrying you is strenuous? Honey, this isn't strenuous; this is perfect. Being able to hold you and kiss you, and not have to fight that rooster makes me stronger than Atlas."

"Maybe so, but I don't want you to get hurt, now put me down. Then you can kiss me and help me into the buggy for our trip home."

Henry smiled. "Yes, ma'am. I'll do what you say only because kissing you would be much more fun if I can pull you up close. Which I can now."

Then, as if to prove his point, Henry sat her on her feet and pulled her right up against him. He captured her lips with his and kissed her much closer to the way he had that morning. When her knees gave out under the feelings he was creating, he held her up and slowly, teasingly gentled the kiss. Finally, when she thought she would pass out from the lack of air and the feelings running through her, he released her lips and lifted her into the buggy. When he climbed up beside her, she almost slid out of the seat, her bones were still so soft and her muscles so much quivering jelly. He pulled her close and wrapped his arm around her, holding the reins in one hand. Then with a snap he headed back down the road toward Creede and the line shack that had been their home for the last week. Only tonight there would be no extra quilts between them, and Hannah couldn't wait to sleep beside her new husband.

HENRY HAD CLIMBED into the buggy and instantly had to grab hold of Hannah. He was tickled by the way his kiss had affected her; she'd been so overwhelmed by his kiss she'd almost slid off the buggy seat. He'd pulled her close to him and she'd just melted against him like it was the only place she wanted to be. He fully understood her feeling. As he breathed in the scent that was completely Hannah, it filled his senses and made him want nothing more than to be immersed in it. When she was near like this, it was all he could do not to just forget that there was a world out there beyond the two of them. Tonight he planned to tell her how he felt. He wanted to whisper those three little words and have her know that he truly meant them with every fiber of his being.

She sighed and he squeezed her tight. "Are you all right, Hannah? Are you cold? There's that bear fur in the back if you need it."

She looked up at him. "Oh no! I'm good, as a matter of fact I'm better than good."

She smiled and leaned close and kissed him on the corner of his mouth. "Thank you for marrying me, Henry."

He pulled her even closer... "No, Hannah, honey. Thank you for marrying me. I'm the one who has found a rare jewel here. What was it the king's mother said in Proverbs? 'A good wife is worth more than rubies.' Or something like that. That's you, Hannah. You're worth more than rubies, diamonds, gold, or silver. That you agreed to be mine makes me the richest man in the world."

They rode on in silence until they entered Creede. Henry drove the buggy past the Nugget and saw Archie and several of his lackeys standing around. One seemed familiar to him, but when he looked back for a second look the man was gone. Maybe it had been his imagination, but he thought it had been Augustus Rayner, the man who'd killed Hannah's sister. He refocused on his lovely wife. "I want to make a couple of stops before we head to the cabin."

Hannah looked up at him with questions in her eye. "I want to stop at Mr. McRae's and get us a couple of dinners. I don't want you to have to cook on our wedding night. I also want to stop at the dry goods and get some sweet corn feed for Bob. He did his job and tonight he'll be sleeping in the lean-to with the cow and horses. So I want to reward him with some special feed."

Hannah squeezed his arm in her hug. "Those both sound like good ideas. I've never actually been in Crowther's Dry Goods; I'll go in with you and look around."

"Darlin', if you want to come everywhere with me today, I'll stop and crow that you're my wife louder than old Bob there ever could."

From the back seat came a disgusted "Brawlk!"

"Nope, Bob, I won't take it back. Our Hannah makes me feel like the strongest man in the world. With her on my arm, not only can I out strut you, I can and will out crow you, too."

Bob clucked like he was disagreeing, and Henry smiled at the giggle that escaped Hannah and the pretty blush that warmed her cheeks and neck.

They stopped in front of Edwin McRae's house and Henry got down and knocked on the door. The man opened and said, "Marshal, thought you were dead."

Henry shook his head. "Everyone today has said that. I'm sorry to disappoint."

"I'm actually glad you aren't dead; maybe you'll be able to help clean up this town."

"Well, I'm trying to do what I was sent here to do, Edwin. Maybe that will help."

"I know you didn't stop by to chat. What can I do for you?"

Henry smiled. "I married Nurse Coppersmith just a little bit ago. I'd like to keep her from having to cook our wedding feast. You wouldn't happen to have two meals handy, would you?"

McRae rubbed his chin. "I normally don't have much in the way of supper on account most miners want a lunch, but

I think I could put together a basket that would feed the two of you pretty good. Might even have a few pieces of apple stack cake left that Miss Bing brought me this morning. Can ya give me about half an hour to make a basket fer ya?"

Henry nodded. "Much obliged. We need to stop by the dry good store, anyway, so we'll be back after that."

"Sounds good; and congratulations on yer nuptials."

Henry smiled. "Thanks, maybe you should think about finding a wife."

McRae smiled. "Might be, I have a thought or two along those lines."

Henry shook his hand and climbed back in the buggy. "He's putting us together a basket, so let's go to the dry goods and then swing by and get our supper."

HANNAH AND HENRY entered Crowther's Dry Goods store. Hannah let go of Henry's arm and started wandering up and down the aisles looking at things. There were several things that the mercantile didn't have and some overlap. There seemed to be more mining and farming goods here than at the mercantile and less in the way of womanly things or household items. She was moving up an aisle looking at canning supplies and kitchen wares when she remembered she'd wanted to ask Henry just what kind of cookware he had in his apartment. She started toward him when she heard and saw Benita Crowther enter the store and make a straight line for Henry. She latched on to his arm like they were courting. "Marshal Wheeler, I'm so relieved that the rumors of your death were wrong. I've been so worried about you."

Henry smiled at her and tried to pull his arm away but

the woman was latched on like a tick on a hound. "Thank you, Miss Crowther. As you can see, I'm fine. I took a bullet to the back but thankfully, I was in good hands."

The girl batted her eyes at him. Hannah wanted to laugh at the silly girl but surprisingly, another part of her wanted to scratch the little flirt's eyes out. "Well, I think to celebrate we should go on a picnic tomorrow. What time will you pick me up?"

Before Henry could open his mouth to answer the forward little leech, Hannah came up behind them. "Benita Crowther, I would appreciate it if you took your hands off my husband."

Benita jerked around as she let go of Henry. "You're married to Nurse Coppersmith? Why didn't you say something?"

Hannah again pulled the woman's attention toward her. "When did he have a chance to? You latched onto him like a saddle on a cowpony the moment you walked in the door."

"I'm sorry, I didn't mean anything. When did you two marry and how come no one knows about it?"

"Henry married me about a half hour ago at Reverend Bing's church. That's why not a lot of people know about it. We stopped here to get some things we need to set up our house together."

The woman sighed. "I don't understand. What is wrong with me? First, it looks like Waylon will be my groom and instead he sends for a mail order bride just like Mr. Jackson. Now you got the Marshal. Why can't I find a husband?"

Hannah started to tell her she came across too desperate for a husband and scared them all off but Henry beat her to saying anything. "You just have to find the right man, Miss Crowther. Hey now, Doctor Thomas isn't married. Maybe he'd be a good match for you. I bet Hannah could mention you to him if you wanted. Why she could even give you an introduction, I bet."

Hannah looked at Henry like he'd grown a third eye. What was that man playing at? Why would he sic this leech onto the doctor? Of course, the Doctor was single. Maybe he would like an introduction to a single woman in town.

Benita looked at her and Hannah sighed. "I'll mention you to him, Benita, but don't get your hopes up too much. He's really very busy, you know."

Benita grabbed her and hugged her. "Oh, thank you, Hannah. I just need a chance. I'll make him a good wife. You'll see."

This was what she'd been afraid of. Henry was a man and lived mostly in Topaz and probably didn't know Benita's reputation for being over-zealous when it came to looking for a husband. Hannah smiled and was relieved when Mr. Crowther came around the corner and handed Henry a sack of sweet corn feed. "Anything else, Marshal?"

He looked at Hannah, "Well, did you see something you need?"

"I'm not sure; maybe I should wait till I see what we have in Topaz first."

Henry nodded. "Nope, that's all this time."

He settled up and they left to get their supper basket and head home for their wedding feast and then the wedding night. Hannah shivered at the thought of finally being able to know Henry as her husband.

13
―――――

Hannah looked at Henry sleeping beside her. The last two weeks had been the best of her life. She and Henry had moved into his apartment over the jail in Topaz and they'd quickly settled into a routine together. Hannah would wake and get up and fix breakfast for them while Henry went out and fed the horses and milked the cow. When he brought the milk in they'd eat together. Some mornings they got out of bed faster than others and Hannah blushed when she thought of those times they lingered in bed. The one thing that made her laugh and irritated Henry was Bob. No matter how sure Henry was that the rooster was locked out of the house at night, they were awakened every morning by Bob sitting on the post at the foot of the bed crowing. Henry couldn't figure out how the rooster was getting in every single morning. Hannah knew it had more to do with who had given her Bob than the bird himself. He was a special bird and so it tickled her but didn't bother her that he could do the impossible.

The other thing was Bob still followed her around. The people of Topaz had even started to laugh and joke about Nurse Hannah and her assistant, Bob Chicken. However, he had come in handy and even helpful a few times. There was the man who'd been more drunk than hurt and tried to get personal with her. Henry had been out with a local rancher chasing rustlers, but Bob had pecked and kicked and beat the man with his large wings till the guy had run out into the street screaming about demonic roosters.

Then there were the little kids who were hurt and scared, and Bob would set and let them hug him or pet him and just cluck lightly to them. Parents of those kids talked about how gentle and kind the oversized rooster was. But mostly they talked about him as Hannah's shadow. Henry had even gone so far as to build a hen house and get six chickens for them and they had eggs every day, but still Bob would end up in the house every morning waking them from the foot of the bed.

Every Wednesday Hannah would hitch her wagon and ride to the clinic and work alongside Doctor Thomas. The man had taken to being out of the clinic himself most other days. More to escape from Benita's attempts at getting him to court her than anything. So they both enjoyed Wednesdays when they could work in the clinic and see to the health of Creede's citizens. Henry rode in with her, his stallion Fury tied behind her buggy. After he'd dropped her off at the clinic, he'd go back into town. Black Jack Ketchem and his deputy had left Creede without a word to anyone. Even Mr. Anders was mad about it since they'd held up a payroll shipment being sent to the mine on their way out of town.

Henry had wanted posters drawn up for them and sent

to every lawman in Colorado, Montana, and Wyoming. But so far all they'd heard were rumors of train and stage coach robberies the two had done. While everyone but Archie and Anders were glad Ketchem was gone, not having a local lawman had made Creede a more dangerous place. Once again women in the area were not going anywhere alone. Henry and Mr. Anders, as well as Reverend Bing, had sent out advertisements for someone to come and take over as sheriff, but so far no one had answered the ads. That left Henry having to spend more time in Creede.

Still, their time together was sweet. Their love for each other was growing and even if Henry hadn't said the words to her yet, Hannah knew he loved her. The one dark spot in her life was Gus. She'd been called to the Golden Nugget twice more over the last two weeks, both times to treat girls that he himself had punished.

So far Henry had not been able to go with her on any of her visits to the Nugget and Bob had never gone inside with her but every time she was finished, Gus would make a comment or try to catch her alone, reminding her that if she breathed a word of who he used to be, she'd pay the price. He also kept making comments about how he bet she was an even better toy than her sister had been and one day he'd have to play with her and see.

Hannah was worried. She had thought about telling both Henry and Doctor Thomas that she wasn't going to see the women at the saloons any more. She had enough with her work in Topaz and seeing all the women who'd come up in a family way lately. There was Beatrice Jameson, Marta Clark, a couple in Topaz, and a few of the miners' wives. Between that and patching up accidents and dealing with illness in and around Topaz, Hannah was busy. She'd talk to

Henry tonight and Doctor Thomas on Wednesday when she went to the clinic. As comfortable as the women were with having her do their doctoring for woman problems, there really wasn't a need for her in Creede. Doctor Thomas could do what was needed without her.

She'd convinced herself that she was going to concentrate on Topaz's citizens and midwifing and put as much distance between her and Gus Reed as possible. She was just getting ready to go to the sheriff's office and meet her husband when Celeste Divine, the first girl she'd patched up after Gus punished her, came into the clinic. "Mrs. Wheeler, I was sent to fetch you; one of the girls is real bad off. This time it wasn't a punishment. Gus said to tell you she's bleeding a whole lot and it ain't her time to bleed."

Hannah nodded and grabbed her bag stuffing extra bandages and some laudanum and witch hazel in the bag as well as her stethoscope and some medicinal alcohol. She climbed in the buggy, motioning for Celeste to climb up beside her. The girl had run all the way from town. "Oh, no, ma'am, I couldn't ride beside you. What would people think?"

"I don't care what they think, Celeste. I'm the one tasked with seeing to your health and well-being, and you've done exhausted yourself coming to get me. Now get up here. We don't have time to argue."

The girl climbed in the buggy and just before Hannah took off, Bob hopped in the back and settled himself on the rear bench. "It's funny how that rooster follows you around, Mrs. Wheeler."

Hannah got her mare heading toward the Nugget. "That's Bob, Celeste, he's a very special rooster."

The girl gave her a puzzled look. "What do you mean?"

Hannah didn't know why but she found herself telling

Celeste all about her guardian angel and the gift of Bob the attack chicken, her protector and chaperone. The girl didn't look like she doubted a word Hannah said but when the tale was told, Celeste said. "But you're married now. Why is he still here?"

"I don't know, Celeste. I guess his job of protecting me isn't over yet. Or maybe he's still here because he has nowhere else to go."

"I know if I was anything but a whore I'd be happy to have a chicken like Bob."

Bob hopped up on the back of the front seat and then into Celeste's lap, letting the innocent minded whore pet him just like he did the little children who needed comfort. Hannah's heart hurt for the young woman beside her. She said a little prayer that this woman would find a way out of the life she was in before that innocence was lost to her cruel profession.

They arrived at the Golden Nugget. Hannah looked around; Mr. Anders wasn't there but Gus was standing on the landing talking to Archie Grady. Something twisted in Hannah's stomach; something about this wasn't right. But maybe it was just the fact that she had to deal yet again with her sister's killer. Gus motioned for her to come with him and she climbed the steps. Archie passed her going down and she felt, more than saw, his eyes travel over her figure in a way that made her feel covered in slime. Gus led her to the door of a room on the far end of the hall. "I had to put her in here. She was screaming so loud earlier that it was upsetting the other girls. She calmed down some when we turned the lights down and covered the windows. But she's bleeding awful bad."

"I'll see what I can do, but if it's as bad as you say you'll probably need to send someone to Bachelor to find Doctor Thomas."

"If we need to we will. Just see what you can do first. If nothing else, give her some medicine so she won't scream anymore."

Hannah nodded and entered the darkened room. There was a single lamp turned down low. She could see the shape of the girl in the bed under the covers. She walked toward the bed unaware of Gus entering behind her and locking the door. "Hey there, I'm Nurse Wheeler. Tell me what's going on with you." As she got nearer the bed she realized that there wasn't a person in the bed but just sheets and blankets arranged to look like a person. Her heart slammed into her chest as she felt Gus grab her from behind "I told you one day I'd see if you were a better plaything than your sister. Archie is sending me to Durango to run the new brothel and you'll be my personal whore from today on. Hannah opened her mouth to scream when something was shoved over her mouth and nose. She caught the scent of ether before everything went black.

HENRY HAD JUST RIDDEN up to the jail in Creede. He was tired; he'd been up at the mine investigating what appeared to be a series of thefts. Turned out that one of the mine engineers was getting a bit forgetful and had misplaced a couple of bags of gold dust. They'd found them in the bottom of his old desk. He'd been putting them there like he used to before they'd gotten a safe that they all used. Henry was tired and hoped that Hannah was ready to head for home. He swung down from the saddle and headed for the office.

Might as well make a pot of coffee while he waited for her to come tell him she was ready to go home.

He'd just reached the boardwalk when he saw Bob running down the street clucking and squawking and beating his wings as he came. A sinking feeling came to him as the bird came close. Bob never was far from Hannah; for him to be acting this way could only mean one thing. Henry's wife was in trouble. "What is it, Bob? Where's Hannah?" The bird turned the minute Henry asked where Hannah was and started back up the street. There beside the Golden Nugget sat her buggy. Bob headed straight for the doors of the saloon. She must have gotten a call to go doctor one of the girls, but Bob wouldn't be worked up if everything was all right. Henry entered the saloon with Bob right on his heels. Archie Grady was sitting at the end of the bar. "Get that nasty bird out of my saloon."

Henry's hands went to the grips of his Colts, slipping off the hammer thongs. "I'm looking for my wife, Archie, and when her rooster and I find her we'll leave. Which room is she in."

"She ain't here. I've been here all day and I ain't seen her at all. Go look somewhere else for her."

Henry's eyes hardened and he walked up to the oily man that he knew had been previously involved in abducting women, including Hannah. He reached down and hauled the human trash up by his shirt front. "I'm going to say this once more, Archie. Her rig's outside so you tell me where she is or I'm going to let her rooster have at you. If he can't loosen your tongue, I'm gonna have a go at ya, and if that don't work I'll throw ya in jail for kidnapping."

The slick dandy smiled. "I told you she ain't here. Why maybe she just got tired of an Eastern Greenhorn pretending to be a real man and found her someone better to run off with."

Henry saw something in his eye that said the man knew where Hannah was and was gloating in the fact that Henry didn't have a clue. Henry pulled him closer and whispered in his ear. "I gave you fair warning; you remember that in about five seconds when you're begging me to stop that rooster." Then he shoved Archie on the floor. "Loosen his tongue, Bob."

With a loud squawk the rooster flew up on the man's chest and started pecking and snapping at Archie's face, neck, and ears. Archie started screaming and trying to cover his eyes but every time he got his hand up, Bob would peck it drawing blood. In less than five minutes, Archie was screaming to get the bird off of him before he lost an eye. Henry saw several patrons and the bartender move to help and drew his Colts. "Anyone move another step and I'll arrest you for obstructing justice. Archie, you better tell me where Hannah is or Bob there will peck your eyes out."

Archie yelled. "She went upstairs with Gus into the last room. That's all I know."

"How long ago?"

"Couple of hours."

Henry called to the rooster. "That's enough, Bob."

The rooster stopped pecking and hopped off Archie with a loud Cock-a doodle-do. Henry and Bob raced up the stairs and down the hall to the room on the end. When he got to the door, it was locked. He didn't even ask for a key, just pulled his right-hand Colt and put a slug into the latch. He kicked the door and came into a completely dark room. He lit the lamp on the table by the door and saw a bed that had sheets piled to look like a body was in the bed. A drag mark where something had hit the edge of the bed and moved it was evident, and there was a scrap of cloth laying on the floor. Henry picked it up and noticed a sticky sweet smell that reminded him of the ether Doctor Thomas used when he and Hannah had to do surgery on someone.

Hannah had been knocked out and kidnapped again. Henry stormed out of the room and pulled both Colts as he came down the stairs. Several men were standing around Archie who was wiping the blood from Bob's attack off his face. Henry pointed the Colts right in Archie's face and pulled back both hammers. "You got about ten seconds to tell me who Gus is and where he's taken my wife before I blow your head off, Mr. Grady."

Archie looked at him and said, "Who is Gus? He's the man my uncle hired to watch over the girls. As for your wife, I told you last I saw she went in the room with Gus. If they aren't up there I don't know what to tell you."

"Stand up. You're under arrest."

"For what?"

"Kidnapping."

"I told you I didn't have anything to do with your wife."

"You know, Archie, I don't believe you. That's twice people who worked with you and for you have kidnapped Hannah, so until I'm sure you're not involved, you're going to jail. When we get there, I think I'll strip you down and tie you to the bed and let Bob peck at some other places besides your face. Maybe then you'll remember where your employee might have taken my wife."

Just then one of the working girls spoke up. "Marshal, I overheard Mrs. Hannah and Gus the last time she came here. She called Gus another name and he told her to keep quiet or he'd hurt her like he'd hurt her sister."

Henry froze and looked at the dark-haired girl. "What name did she call him, miss?"

His blood ran cold when she said, "Augustus, she called him Augustus something."

"Rayner?"

"Yes, that was the name."

He looked at Archie. "Augustus Rayner is a killer with a bounty on his head in New York. Last chance, Archie, where did he take Hannah?"

Archie smiled. "I have no idea, but it doesn't sound too good for you, does it? Reckon you'll be a widower soon."

Henry grabbed the man by the shirt and tossed him halfway across the bar. "Get moving, you're going to jail and this time your uncle won't be able to buy your way out."

Archie might have been inclined to try and run but Bob was on his heels the whole way, squawking and pecking. Once he was locked up, Henry turned to go see if he could find a trail to follow. As he came out of the back of the jail where the cells were, he saw a lady with graying auburn hair standing in front of his desk. "Hello, Marshal Wheeler. I don't have time to be subtle about this so I hope you can take the shock.

"My name is Penny and I'm a messenger and guardian sent from God."

Henry wanted to discard the woman as crazy and get on with looking for Hannah but when she started to glow like the sun he stopped in shock. The light dimmed enough that he could see the woman. "Augustus Rayner has your wife tied over the back of a horse he's leading up the mountain pass to Durango. If I were you, I'd make haste to catch them before he stops for the night. He plans to violate her like he did her sister before he killed her."

Henry didn't say a word, just detoured to the desk and pulled a box of shells for his Colts and rifle from the drawer and headed out, slipping the box in his saddle bags. He turned to see the woman setting Bob on the saddle bags. "Take Bob with you; his job isn't complete."

Henry nodded, "Thank you, Penny."

"Don't thank me yet, boy, go save our girl first."

Henry nodded and kicked Fury into a full gallop. He didn't look back but if he had he would have seen Penny fade from existence behind him.

14

Hannah woke to find herself tied over the back of a horse, her head pounding from the ether used to knock her out. She instantly remembered what had happened. Her sister's killer had tricked her, and then knocked her out and tied her over the horse she was on. He was sitting on another and leading the one she was secured to. There was a rope tying her hands to one stirrup and she figured her feet were tied to the other one. They were somewhere in the mountains. She sucked in as large a breath as she could and screamed. Augustus laughed. "I see you finally woke up. Well, scream all you want; we're high up in the mountains and there ain't no one here to hear you."

She took a deep breath to scream again when suddenly Penny was beside her on a black horse with a white blaze down it's forehead. "He's right; there's no one here that can hear you."

"Penny, can you help me?" Hannah whispered.

The woman shook her head. "I'm not allowed to show myself to anyone but you and now Henry, too. But that's it.

I'm here to give you courage, my dear. Your husband is on his way and he has Bob with him. They aren't slowed down by having to lead a horse so they should catch up to you in about an hour. You just stay strong and preserve your strength."

The woman started to fade and Hannah cried quietly, "Please don't leave me alone."

The woman came back to the same density she'd been earlier. "Lightning and I will stay with you as long as we can, my dear. But I'm not allowed to interfere with Augustus. Whatever happens will be up to you and Henry and Augustus."

Hannah nodded, "I understand. It's just I'm afraid."

"I know, dear. I remember when I was in your situation. It was the most afraid I'd ever been in my life."

"But you survived it?"

"I did. But only because God led Nate to me. He helped me survive what was done to me and his love helped heal me."

Hannah couldn't stop the tears that flowed down her face. "Are you telling me I'm going to have to endure what Augustus has threatened?"

"I don't know, dear. I've told your husband how to find you. If he gets here in time; then no, but I don't know the future. I only know what the Boss lets me know."

"Is there nothing you can do to help us?"

"I can't do anything that will reveal me to anyone but you and Henry."

"Penny, you said if I need something from you to just call out and ask, right?"

"Yes, dear, and as long as it doesn't violate the rules the Boss gave me, I'll do what I can."

"That thing you did to get me to the Golden Nugget to

help Celeste; could you do that for Henry? To get him here faster?"

Penny thought for a second. "I believe I can. It doesn't violate the rules I was given."

"Will you please bring my husband and Bob to me, Penny?"

The temporary angel smiled. "He'll be here faster than you can doubt it will happen, my dear."

Then the woman and horse were gone.

"What are you mumbling about back there?"

"Nothing that would interest you. Augustus Rayner. I'm just praying and asking God to save me."

Augustus laughed. "Well save your breath. Ain't no one going to save you. You belong to me now."

HENRY RACED UP THE MOUNTAIN. He was pushing Fury as hard as he could, but he knew soon he'd have to slow down or risk killing his horse. Just when he was thinking about it, the angel appeared beside him on a big, black horse. "You're not going to make it in time to keep her from being hurt, Henry. Not on your own. I need you to give me your reins, please, and trust me."

Henry looked at the woman and realized all at once who she was. This woman's portrait hung over the fireplace at the Dueling N's Ranch in Redemption, New Mexico. This was Nathan's grandmother, Penny Ryder, wife to Nugget Nate Ryder. "Mrs. Ryder, I trusted your grandson with my life several times; I believe I can trust you, too." He handed her Fury's reins. She smiled at him, "Would you mind holding on to Bob and maybe your saddle horn? We're going to move at angelic speed."

Henry reached behind him and scooped up the rooster and held him tight against his chest. The rooster tucked his head under his wing and became very still. Henry reached his other hand and twisted it in a handful of Fury's mane and grabbed the saddle horn. Before he knew what to think, they were thundering through the sky, moving faster than any horse naturally could; yet Fury wasn't even running, just a gentle trot was the motion Henry felt in his faithful mount.

Soon he could see two horses on the ground just a short way ahead of them. Penny led them closer to the ground and Fury's pace increased from a trot to a full gallop just as his feet hit the ground. Penny handed the reins back to Henry. "That's all I can do. The rest is up to you, Marshal."

"Thank you."

The woman nodded and then faded away. Henry could see that Hannah was tied over the saddle and her horse was being led by Augustus. He let go of Bob who clucked and hopped on his shoulder and then to the back of the saddle. He leaned forward giving Fury his head and the magnificent golden palomino poured on speed. How Rayner couldn't hear the thundering of his hooves, Henry couldn't understand; but the big stallion drew even with the mare his wife was tied to. Henry got the horses as close together as he could, pulled his left leg across the saddle and stood with it in the right stirrup, and then vaulted over to land right behind his wife on her mount. He wrapped his hand in the horse's mane, leaned to the left, pulled his bowie knife, and cut the rawhide strip tying her hands to the saddle. Then he leaned right and cut her feet loose. He stuck the knife back in his belt and hauled Hannah upright. When he got her sitting upright on the horse, he kissed the back of her neck, handed her the bowie knife, and motioned for her to cut the lead rope going to Rayner's mount. She nodded and leaned as far forward as she could and quickly sliced the lead rope in two. Henry pulled back on the handful of mane in his fist and the horse slowed to a stop. He'd just swung Hannah to the ground when Rayner realized the lead rope had gone slack and looked back. When he saw Hannah on the ground, he turned to fire at Henry. Just as he drew a bead, Fury drew up beside Rayner and there came a super loud COCK-A-DOODLE-DO! Rayner's head jerked to the sight of Bob standing tall in the saddle with both wings flapping furiously. The rooster launched itself at the outlaw and caught him square in the face with his spurs. Rayner screamed and fell off his horse, rolling to try to get away from the rooster that was scratching and pecking away at him. Before anyone could move or shout, the rooster let go of the man as he rolled off the side of the cliff. There was a terrible scream and then silence.

Henry got down and Hannah flew into his arms. "I knew you'd come."

Henry pulled her into his arms and kissed her. When he came up for air, he said, "Hannah, never doubt that I'll come for you. I'll always come for you. I love you, sweetheart, more than I ever thought I could love anyone.

Hannah smiled. "I know, darling, and I love you, too." Bob strutted up to them clucking all the way. "Yes, Bob, I love you, too. Thank you for helping to save me."

The rooster clucked and crowed as if to say, "Think nothing of it, ma'am, just doing my job."

Henry looked down at the rooster, too. "Yes, Bob, thank you for your help. I believe you saved my life today as well. I reckon that makes you my deputy now, don't it? The rooster looked sideways at Henry and then puffed up his chest with a strong Cock-a-doodle-do! "No, I'm not giving you a badge. Where would you wear it anyway?"

Henry walked over to the edge where Rayner had fallen over and looked in the deepening twilight. He couldn't see anything but he doubted that the killer could have survived the fall. He collected Rayner's horse and the mare that Hannah had been tied to. Then he pulled a length of coiled lasso out of his saddle bags and fashioned a new lead rope for the mare and helped Hannah up onto the horse Rayner had been riding. After placing Bob on the mare's saddle he climbed onto Fury. Looking at his wife and then back at the rooster, Henry said, "Let's go home."

EPILOGUE

Henry lay in bed watching Hannah sleep. She'd clung to him all night, even in her sleep and he'd had to soothe her through nightmares several times. He'd talked to Doctor Thomas when they'd returned and he'd checked Hannah over and declared she was physically okay. He had given Henry some medicine to help her sleep and warned him it might take a while for her to get over the terror of being kidnapped a second time. He would hold her and soothe her as often as he needed to. He watched her as his heart filled with his love for her.

She opened her eyes and smiled at him, snuggling closer. "Good morning, Marshal Wheeler."

"Good morning, Nurse Wheeler."

She leaned up and kissed him. "Have you been awake long?"

Henry shook his head. "Not too long."

"What were you doing? Watching me sleep?"

He nodded and then smiled. "Yes, and thinking."

"About what?"

He stroked her cheek. "This is going to sound crazy but I was thinking I owed Augustus Rayner thanks."

She frowned. "Why would you owe that killer thanks?"

Henry looked her straight in the eye. "Because he kept me from making the biggest mistake in my life. If not for him I'd have married your sister instead of the real love of my life.

"Well, I'm not sure I agree you owe him thanks as much as you owe Esther thanks. I guess we owe Ketchem thanks as well then. For shooting you in the back and trapping us together for a week."

"Maybe we do. But there is one thing all of this has taught me."

She snuggled closer, her hands going around his body pulling him as close as possible "What has it taught you?"

"That often the person you're looking for is right in front of you the whole time you were searching for her, only you don't realize it till it's almost too late."

"But you did realize it, Henry, and we have a lifetime to love each other."

He nodded and then proceeded to show her just how he planned to love her for the rest of their life.

Later, as they lay in each other's arms there was a sudden weight on the foot of the bed and a loud COCK-A-DOODLE-DO!

Henry sighed. "Do you think if you asked, Mrs. Ryder would come and take her rooster back with her?"

Hannah giggled. "I don't think so. I'm pretty sure Bob will be with us till his job here is done."

"I was afraid you'd say that."

He looked at the bird sitting at the end of the bed. "Fine, Bob, you can stay but you've got to stop letting yourself in the house."

The rooster turned his head to the right and looked at Henry with his right eye, then tilted it to the left and looked at Henry with the left eye. Then he clucked several times as if to say, "Deal with it. I'm right where I'm supposed to be." Henry just shrugged and then let himself get lost in his wife's lips once more.

The End.

ABOUT THE AUTHOR

George McVey always wanted to be a superhero; sadly, no radioactive storms or animals have been a part of his life. One day while spinning a tall tale for his family, some suggested once again that with all his experiences in ministry, and his imagination, he should be writing books. This time it was like lightning struck him and he decided, *why not?*

Since then George has been hard at work using his creative imagination and writing several books. He's still adding to his bibliography to this day.

George lives in the wonderful state of Almost Heaven, West Virginia. A few years ago, he moved from a single-family home to a deluxe apartment in the sky, well the fourth floor anyway. He lives with his wife of thirty years and a service dog named Daisy Mae. He is visited often by his three children and two grandsons.

If you ever come to visit him, you will probably find him sitting in his lazy boy recliner or at his desk in the corner office working on some writing project. If it's not a teaching book, then it's a novel. If he isn't working on a novel, then he will be working either on a short story or blog post. If he isn't doing either of those then he is either asleep or eating, his other two favorite past times.

You can reach him by email at pastor.george.mcvey@gmail.com. You can also find out more about his books, get a free book, or join his beta readers team to help make the books he writes better at his website georgemcvey.weebly.com. You can also connect with George on Facebook at his author page https://www.facebook.com/George-H-Mcvey-557196424346233.

If you would like to read good clean books, then you might find any or all these Facebook Readers Groups helpful. You can meet authors and talk with them and other readers about their books there. Christian Indie Authors and Readers group, Sweet Wild West Readers Group, and Pioneer Hearts Readers groups. George is part of all three.

Join the Silverpines's Readers Group on Facebook to stay caught up on all the Silverpines's action and talk with other fans of the series and authors.

~

ALSO BY GEORGE MCVEY

Join George's newsletter and receive a FREE copy of Grandpa Mac's Tall Tales. This exclusive short story collection is only available when you sign up for the newsletter. Sign up online and check out George's other books at georgemcvey.weebly.com

WHAT'S NEXT FOR COWBOYS AND ANGELS

Have a blast hanging out in Creede, Colorado? There's more where that came from. Visit www.sarajolene.com/cowboys-angels-first-chapter **for a sneak peek of what's next in the Cowboys and Angels series.**

Made in the USA
Columbia, SC
21 March 2022

57969674R00081